Droving down the Cooper

'Let's go bush,' and those words sparked a journey for two adventurous city kids under the spell of Banjo Paterson, and his tales of horses and men in the Australian outback.

Col Hood's story unfolds, filled with discovery, bush wisdom and the people who made his life. Horse traders, blacksmiths, master leatherworkers and above all the horses.

In his introduction to this book, Col invites the reader to 'ride stirrup to stirrup' with him while he tells his stories.

Mad if you don't.

Col Hood was one of the first two saddlemakers in Australia to build the western saddle, and his skill in saddlemaking brought him fame in the world of horsemen. He has also bred fine Quarter Horses and, is widely known as a brilliant raconteur.

Author 22, back in the stock saddle days, mid-50s.

Droving down the Cooper

A Saddlemaker's Yarns

Col Hood

ROSENBERG

DEDICATION

This book is dedicated to the memory of people who were important in
my life:

to my mother, for having the foresight to see that I was born in the country;
to my brother Alan, who 'fathered' me when our dad was away at the war;
to Neville Page, the intrepid Spinifex Mick;
to John G. Chirnside, my teacher, mentor and friend;
and, in particular, to my soul mate, my beloved Mary.

First published in Australia in 2010
by Rosenberg Publishing Pty Ltd
PO Box 6125, Dural Delivery Centre NSW 2158
Phone: 61 2 9654 1502 Fax: 61 2 9654 1338
Email: rosenbergpub@smartchat.net.au
Web: www.rosenbergpub.com.au

National Library of Australia Cataloguing-in-Publication entry

Author: Hood, Col.

Title: Droving down the Cooper : a saddlemaker's yarns / Col Hood.

Edition: 1st ed.

ISBN: 9781877058950 (pbk.)

Notes: Includes index.

Subjects: Hood, Col—Journeys—Australia.
Men—Australia—Biography.

Dewey Number: 920.710994

Edited by Helen Young
Cover photo by Quinn Rooney (Getty Images)

Printed in China by Everbest Printing Co Limited

CONTENTS

Introduction

The first horse in my life I called Long Tom; I bought him with the money I saved when I started an apprenticeship at fifteen. Tom set me off on a journey that's always been associated with horses, their riders and their tackle, and that led me to become a very well known western saddlemaker.

I was riding a horse when I first met Big Nev, an adventurous kid like myself, and we discovered that we shared the same dream – to head for the outback and go 'droving down the Cooper, where the western drovers go'. Banjo Paterson's poem 'Clancy of the Overflow' had caught us and held us. Read it, and I think you'll understand how it blew the minds of a couple of horse-mad kids dying to get out of the city.

I've done a lot of things. Some of the things I've done were wrong, and sometimes I've even done 'em twice. Perfect I am not, but I tell it the way it is.

So if you'd like to swing into the saddle we can take a ride, stirrup to stirrup, while I tell you the way it was.

Col Hood
Balmattum, 2009

Acknowledgments

Here's a thank you to all those fine horsemen and artists who have guided and believed in me through the years … to that great horseman, Max McTaggart, for his unflagging support, and to the memory of superb outback artist Hugh Sawrey, a friend and mentor, and thanks to his wife Gill. For a lifetime of friendship and support I owe much to my sister, Val, who has encouraged me in writing this book and all my other endeavours.

I'd also like to mention the cowgirls, who were always among my best customers. They worked, saved their money for one of my saddles, paid promptly, left happy and twenty years later they brought back their daughters. In every way, they have been an adornment to western riding

Clancy of The Overflow

A.B. "Banjo" Paterson

I had written him a letter which I had, for want of better
  Knowledge, sent to where I met him down the Lachlan, years ago,
He was shearing when I knew him, so I sent the letter to him,
  Just "on spec", addressed as follows: "Clancy, of The Overflow".

And an answer came directed in a writing unexpected,
  (And I think the same was written in a thumbnail dipped in tar)
'Twas his shearing mate who wrote it, and verbatim I will quote it:
  "Clancy's gone to Queensland droving, and we don't know where he
    are."

In my wild erratic fancy visions come to me of Clancy
  Gone a-droving "down the Cooper" where the western drovers go;
As the stock are slowly stringing, Clancy rides behind them singing,
  For the drover's life has pleasures that the townsfolk never know.

And the bush hath friends to meet him, and their kindly voices greet
  him
  In the murmur of the breezes and the river on its bars,
And he sees the vision splendid of the sunlit plains extended,
  And at night the wondrous glory of the everlasting stars.

I am sitting in my dingy little office, where a stingy
  Ray of sunlight struggles feebly down between the houses tall,
And the foetid air and gritty of the dusty, dirty city
  Through the open window floating, spreads its foulness over all.

And in place of lowing cattle, I can hear the fiendish rattle
  Of the tramways and the buses making hurry down the street,
And the language uninviting of the gutter children fighting,
  Comes fitfully and faintly through the ceaseless tramp of feet.

And the hurrying people daunt me, and their pallid faces haunt me
  As they shoulder one another in their rush and nervous haste,
With their eager eyes and greedy, and their stunted forms and weedy,
  For townsfolk have no time to grow, they have no time to waste.

And I somehow fancy that I'd like to change with Clancy,
  Like to take a turn at droving where the seasons come and go,
While he faced the round eternal of the cashbook and the journal -
  But I doubt he'd suit the office, Clancy, of "The Overflow".

The Bulletin, 21 December 1889.

CHAPTER 1

Droving down the Cooper

I've got a soft spot for Windorah. It was in the Windorah pub that I got the job that Banjo Paterson had inspired me to do. I went 'droving down the Cooper', just as he'd written. My mate Bill and I had downed a few beers, talked cattle, and kept our ears open for any talk of a job. We were in luck … the bloke at the end of the bar was a contract musterer looking for men to muster one of the big downs stations, South Galway I think. He took us on.

The next day we climbed onto the works truck with our saddles and swags and headed out to the cattle camp to join the crew. And there they were, tall lean men in their iconic Australian moleskins, or their still new R.M. Williams jeans. They were all wearing elastic-sided boots and long-necked Willoughby spurs, spring-side leggings and big Akubra hats with a dent in front, called the Kimberly bash. Each stockman carried a stock whip and had on his belt a knife pouch, a watch pouch and a pouch for the Vestas, a tin box of wax matches. Most all of these stockmen smoked, they rolled their own. It made me smile in a work camp late at night to hear the frantic scratching of a wax match on the roughened bottom of the match tin. It'd be some old stockman lighting the quirlie he'd just rolled. I guess smoking was the only vice for these tough weatherbeaten, work-hardened men, except for whisky and women of the night.

We were up and dressed before sunrise the next day and ate breakfast as the plant horses were being run into camp.

We were allotted a horse, and in that hard country we'd have a change of horses at midday. So we saddled up and waited for orders from the foreman.

Bill and I were put into a crew of good experienced stockmen. We swept through the country making sure not to miss a wash-out or a dense clump of scrub that might hold a knot of beasts. Those open-range cattle rarely see a human being, and even when you're on horseback they will 'high tail it'. You might come across a small bunch; they would startle, fling their heads in the air, give a snort, and be off at full run with one of us in hot pursuit. The aim was to try and slow them down and swing them towards the main mob that was building along the centre of the paddock – and these paddocks were the size of a small country.

Mulga spiders would build big heavy webs between the trees and sit there just at face height when you are on horseback. At full clip you'd gallop into these webs, and sort of twist your body around and try to see if these huge grey spiders had hit the ground or were maybe somewhere on your person. At the end of the day we were covered in spider webs.

At the end of the muster a large number of cattle were formed into a tight mob called a circle, and held there by stockmen. It was time for the camp drafter to cut out the cattle that were to go to the rail. This top cattleman rode the camp horse quietly into the circle and, one at a time, he drafted out the beasts that were to take the long walk. As each animal was walked out it was taken by stockmen called tailing men, who had the task of hurrying the beast to a second round camp that was building up nearby. It was fast and exacting work for both stockmen and horses – the camp horse was changed after the action of a hundred or so beasts.

By the time the boss drover took delivery of them, the stockmen had built a mob of close to a thousand head. They had a long, hot walk ahead of them – it would be 20 days before they reached Quilpie.

It was good to work with such skilled stockmen on good horses. Bill and I were just a few days in that cattle camp but it was a great experience. With what I had learned back in Wilcannia and what I'd picked up here I was feeling good, feeling like a stockman.

We weren't under contract to the station so we joined up with the drovers. This was our first real job as cattle drovers and I was looking forward to the experience. I just wanted to live the life of being in the middle of this vast open land with only your horse, the other drovers and a huge mob of cattle.

The cattle crew consisted of the boss drover Bert, another much older and very weather-beaten old hand named Charlie, and I made up the third. Bert's brother Jim was the camp cook, and Bill cracked the job of horse tailer and cook's roustabout. His job, considered cushy, was to keep together and run the fifty or sixty workhorses to the next camp each day. He'd hobble and bell a number of them at night, and it was also his job to catch and saddle the night horses we would ride on night watch. He'd gather the workhorses (called the plant) in the mornings before sun up, and each of us would catch and saddle the horse we would be riding all that day.

Each drover would be allotted four or five horses, and these would be ridden in rotation. Occasionally you'd draw a rogue, and every four or five days this barrel of dynamite would come up. Usually once you were in the saddle these horses were all right, but those first few bucks in the semi-dark of a crisp outback morning would sure shake you up. But that was all in a day's work.

The days would start like this – Clang, clang, clang, 'C'mon, it's bloody near five o'clock, yer breakfast's ready,' from Jim the cook. You didn't linger a minute too long in your swag or you'd get a sharp 'Out of there you lazy bugger, you'll get bloody bed sores.' You'd wash and have a cup of tea, and while we were having a good hot breakfast the horse tailer would be running the horses in. Straight after breakfast we'd roll our swags and throw them onto the cook wagon and the day's work started.

We'd catch and saddle the horse of the day, fill the canvas water bags we carried around the horse's neck and, with a bit of damper and salt beef in our saddlebag for mid-day break, we'd ride out and take the mob from the drover who had been on the last watch of the night. He'd have a wash and a quick breakfast, saddle his day horse, roll his swag and catch up with the mob. Depending on the type of country, the boss might call him in and just let the cattle graze until we were ready to put them together and poke on down the trail.

Cattle being walked any distance in a large mob soon work out their own pecking order. The drovers have to keep their eyes open, but they soon get to know the cattle. The ones that started off in the lead are always in the lead; the lazy slugs, always under the whip and eating dust, will duck back at any time, stop and start to graze, The curious ones are on the flanks; they can't wait to wander off for a look…and stay there. Apart from that and a few other incidents, each day was just a ride in the park.

As soon as the mob was on the move each day, the horse tailer would catch the wagon horses, help the cook break camp, help load the wagon, and harness the team. Then he'd gather the plant horses together and accompany the cook wagon to the next stop, where he'd help to set up for the night camp.

We drovers would be poking the cattle along at an easy but ground-covering pace. Bert, the boss drover, would be directing them as we brought up the rear, trying to keep the mob looking neat as they plodded on, mile after mile. The stock routes were many miles wide and passed through some huge cattle stations – we could be three days crossing just one property. We were required to send telegrams ahead to let them know when we would be coming through.

The cattle would be rested for a few hours in the hottest

part of the day when they'd be allowed to graze or just lie about. All we had to do was relax, have lunch, maybe build a fire and make a cup of tea and keep one eye on the mob to make sure they didn't stray too far. When the break was over and the boss started to move the cattle, you'd mount up and get on with easing or pushing the mob until they were on the night camp, where one or two drovers would ride around the beasts settling them down. We would talk and sing softly to them until the majority of them were lying down contentedly chewing their cud.

One man would stay until the first watch came on, then that drover could ride into camp, unsaddle his horse, dry its back and hand it over to the horse tailer. A splash wash, evening meal, a cup or two of tea, a smoke and the night was his own.

You'd be dead asleep in your swag when, at some ungodly hour, you'd be woken to do your night shift. You'd sleepily mount your night horse and spend the next two hours quietly riding around the mob, softly talking and singing to them until the next watch took over. Riding there in such peace, quietly singing old favourites like 'Red River Valley' or 'Old Faithful', I'd sometimes think how much better the world would be if we could keep crowds of humans calm by softly singing to them.

Everything would run smoothly if the weather was good, but you can have a raging thunder storm at night and that puts all the cattle on their feet and restless. With your hat pulled low and collar turned up you'd ride around the mob, talking to reassure them. I remember it being so dark that the only time I could see the cattle was when there was a lightning flash, and in its eerie brightness maybe I'd see a long trail of cattle drifting off into the night. I'd canter the night horse softly around and ease the wanderers back in, and the next flash would reveal another lot drifting out the other side. The important thing was for me to hold them together until my watch was over. I was learning, and this was all experience.

Most days were spent just looking at the north end of the cattle as they trudged relentlessly southward towards Quilpie, but at times there was other work to do, necessary jobs like killing a beast and helping the cook butcher and salt the meat. On this, my first real droving trip, it was my job to ride into the mob on a young, not yet sour saddle horse, select the right beast and shoot it in the head. It was always said that you can fire a rifle off any horse…at least once. But by quietly shooting over the rump of a good young unspoiled horse, you will avoid having the horse blow up under you. I didn't mind that job at all because I knew what I was doing, and I knew there would be good tender undercut steak at the very next meal, and fresh meat for a day or so. The undercut is the section of meat along the backbone and under the ribs, the one cut you can cook and eat straight away.

There's more to droving than just tailing the mob and watching your shadow. Every now and then the cattle would have to be counted This job is best done as you pass through a gate in a fence, or you can run the mob through a set of yards. But if the need arose they would have to be counted in open country. The boss would sit on a horse and we would string the cattle out in single file past him while he counted them in twenties, and marked each 'score' in a note pad. Heaven help you if you ran them through too fast or let any slip behind him – those old boss drovers were strict taskmasters. I always thought the horse tailer had it easy, but Bill got more than he expected one day when a couple of good-looking young brumby colts about fifteen hands high got in with the saddle horses. Knowing there was a set of government yards not far up ahead, the boss told the horse tailer to run all the horses in. He wanted the two brumbies, but if the ranger saw them in the mob he'd shoot them for sure; the plan was to run the brumbies up the race, brand and castrate them, and then they were his.

That same morning, as usual, I saw the cook wagon and plant horses go past the cattle; later in the morning we passed the set of yards and I saw Bill's horse tied to the stockyard fence. There was Bill in the stockyard race with an axe and a hand saw, with blood and bits of horse everywhere. One of the two brumbies had reared over backwards in the race and broken its back. The boss had shot the injured horse and Bill's job was to cut it up and haul it out. We had no tractor, no way was Jim going to use his harness horses to haul out a dead horse, and you don't leave a dead horse in a set of government yards. You could call it a learning experience; not one he'd hoped for, but Bill got the job done anyway.

Out there a learning experience can happen when you least expect it. On one particular day the weather was hot and, as usual, we had the cattle on the track well before the sun rose, intending to water the mob at a government bore about mid-day. The bore tank was dry when we got there, and there was no chance of making the windmill work. The next water was a full day's walk ahead, and all we could do in the meantime was to drive them onwards towards the night camp site.

We had about a quarter of a mile to go to the wagon and cook tent when the cattle, dog-tired and thirsty, decided that this was far enough, they were going no further. No amount of flogging with stockwhips was going to move them – you'd get two on their feet and ten more would lie down. Jim the cook and Bill were not very happy that evening when the boss rode over and told them to break camp and move the wagon, the tent and the horses back to where the cattle had stopped, but with the camp set up and a new fire, the cook soon had a meal cooked and the horse tailer had the night horses saddled. The cattle were quiet that night and we were ready for a very early start next morning.

It was close to pitch black when we broke camp. We had a long walk ahead of us to the next water, and we had covered a good distance before sun up. The cattle would have a break in the hottest part of the day and then it would be back on the track. Being on a stock route, we knew there was another government bore up ahead.

It was mid afternoon when the cattle got the smell of the water. Well before we knew it, the leaders started to string out at an ambling trot, ears cupped and noses sniffing the air. Our job was to control this and avoid a headlong rush, so we rode on the flanks and were able to string them out over about five miles.

The leaders hit the trough and began drinking thirstily. As more cattle got there the troughs couldn't replenish themselves quickly enough and very soon the cattle were licking the dry metal of the troughs. The bulk of the mob were milling around frantically, bellowing for water. Things were looking dicey.

Suddenly the sky, which had been slowly clouding over, miraculously opened up with a downpour that filled all the surface depressions, and with water from these gilgais the cattle were getting a drink. But things still didn't look so good for us. Lightning was striking the ground all around, and the only thing taller than us horsemen was the windmill. I was glad to see the storm pass over, but our problems weren't over yet – the cattle were still thirsty, and they'd drunk all the ground water. Then a second miracle happened that afternoon – the storm turned around and went over us again. It was a very contented mob of cattle we put on camp that evening.

I did have another experience of a desperate rush for water much later when I was droving down the Cooper with a mob of bullocks. By ten o'clock one morning my water bag was empty, and by dinner camp I badly needed a drink. The cattle were settling in for a rest when I spotted a small sink hole of water in the dry creek-bed up ahead of me. I went to ease my horse towards that inviting sight, but the cattle got a whiff of it at the same time. I dug in the spurs and was at full gallop but the bullocks hit a run as they bellowed and roared along the coolabah-lined creek bed. I leapt from the saddle at full gallop and dived for the sinkhole but a couple of hundred frantic bellowing beef cattle beat me by a split second. I didn't get a drink for another six or seven hours. You learn from these experiences; I guess something sunk in.

Bert was a good cattleman and a good boss to learn from, even if only by observation, as we were supposed to be experienced drovers. He didn't take dills lightly; I guess he woke to Bill and me as city kids, it stood out a bit, but we worked hard and he never spoke to us in a derogatory manner. He was straight, he paid well and on time, and we respected him.

We learnt the ways of the bush talking around the campfire. That was the time, too, after the evening meal when we would read, write a letter or do a bit of handcraft. I remember some of the cattlemen I worked with doing excellent horse and cattle-dog portraits by scratching into the painted surface of a tobacco tin with a pocket-knife. I would almost call it 'drovers' scrimshaw'; some were works of art. Some men would plait bridles from the old hay band, others would use the sharp edges of broken beer bottles to scrape bits of mulga into curios like boomerangs. I'd occasionally sketch a steer or a horse, but then again, I had a camera in my saddlebag.

Those stockmen from half a century ago were a breed of their own. They came from the bush, took the first job they were offered, and stayed on forever. They did their jobs well and with an inner pride; they worked, drank and fought hard. They were tough, but they didn't mind helping a kid and showing him the ropes. They all wore moleskins or R.M. Williams jeans, elastic-sided Cuban heeled boots and springside leggings, which they'd clip around the ankles for some reason, and of course the big Akubra with the Kimberly bash. In their working world there was no such thing as workplace safety regulations … you did it right or risked dying.

Living on beef, damper, spuds and onions, we looked forward to something sweet, so it was damper and treacle, dumplings and treacle, rice and treacle or the good old favourite, 'blancmange'. This outback delicacy, pronounced 'blomonge,' was made with powdered milk, water and corn flour plus I don't know what else. It was served up in a tin plate and laced with treacle. Together with a cup of black tea this would top off a good day's work.

One evening after dinner Bert was voicing his disdain for the channel country – he and his brother Jim were from the granite way up north – and this time he was cutting loose about the blue-grey discoloured ground water on these black soil plains. 'I'm sick of this channel country,' he snorted, 'blue water, look at this! Blue tea, and' – holding out his serving of blancmange – 'blue-bloody-monge.'

Every now and then there would be a bit of action. From the side and behind you would hear a low growling bellow and there would be a huge unbranded bull about the size of a small bus coming relentlessly towards the mob. First thing to do was to ride in front of it and try to turn it away, using your stockwhip to swipe it around the ears and face; very hard to do, especially if you had cows in the mob. If the bull did get past you, then you would keep it moving by getting behind it and, with your whip, driving it into a gallop and chasing it out of the mob a mile or two across the plain. Some drovers carried a six-gun and they'd shoot the beast dead on the spot. I had to be content to flog 'em across the plain with a stockwhip.

When stock inspectors stopped us to check the health of

the cattle, we'd have to hold them or walk them past to be inspected for pleuro-pneumonia. This must have been very contagious, because if the inspector said a beast had it then that beast had to be shot and its carcase burned. That meant one of us would have to stay back, gather wood together, start a fire and keep piling on scrub-wood until the beast was burned – or the inspector was gone.

When we arrived at Quilpie common, the boss rode into town and hired some extra hands to help to graze the cattle until it was time to load them onto the train. It was a couple of days before we were to load and, with the extra hands watching the cattle, I was able to take a break and ride into town. The boss and I had ridden in to arrange for delivery of the cattle and to pay us off, when he spotted one of the workers he had hired to look after the cattle. With a short sprint, a well-aimed elastic-sided boot straight up the backside and a tirade of expletives he sent that lazy good-for-nothing back to the cattle very smartly.

We were given the go-ahead to gather the cattle and walk them the couple of miles to the loading yards. All was going well, we had crossed the track and were moving them around to the yards, when the engine driver decided to move the train. The cattle were a little spooky at the sight of this fire-breathing monster, but they were behaving themselves until the train hit the part where the cattle had crossed the track. The driving wheels hit the wet cow plop and spun at high speed and the train let out a gigantic roar as the engine raced. The cattle didn't like that at all and, wide-eyed, they rushed in the opposite direction, the same distance we had just walked them. We gathered the mob together, walked them back again, and with a lot of whooping and hollering we loaded them onto the train.

And that was the end of my first droving job.

With the job finished and the train load of cattle gone, we figured we needed a shower and a good bed, so we stayed the night in the local boarding house. Next morning over breakfast, when I raised the subject of what we were going to do next, Bill said he was catching the next train to Brisbane. Maybe he didn't take to droving, or perhaps this young ladies' man had a passion for one of the waitresses we'd chatted up. I had been looking forward to working with Bill on another droving trip; instead of that I rode the mail truck back to Windorah with one of the drovers I had worked with.

There was a big difference in Windorah when I returned – while I was away the pub had burned down. Undaunted, the publican was serving big brown bottles from a cooler in a tin garage. We all sat under a couple of big old gum trees, talked cattle, work and the heat as we drank a cold beer or two. It was Slim Dusty's 'Pub with no Beer' in reverse; this was the 'beer with no pub'.

I camped that night on the outskirts of town, and next day took a job with a contract mustering crew and stayed on the mustering camp with the rest of the men. This is where it ceased being a fun adventure and became a serious job

I wasn't there to learn, I was there to do a job, but the older stockmen would always guide you and put you on the right track. There was one stockman, a strange sort of bloke, who intimated he had a name or two but for some reason had opted for anonymity. Nameless perhaps, but he was a good stockman. We were shepherding out a mob of newly mustered cattle for the night, and I was trailing a small band that had sneaked off in the dark. There were tracks in the red sandy soil of about twenty cattle heading determinedly north, and I was about to follow when that same stockman said, 'See that single track heading off to the right?' I nodded. 'She stopped for some reason and now she's taken a short cut to catch up with the rest of the mob. We'll follow her.' We took the same short cut and caught up with the cattle in no time. That's one way of learning, through other people's experience; other times you learn by what you've experienced yourself.

Experience comes from doing it, even if it's wrong. While out mustering one time, I was trailing a flighty little bunch of cattle when they spotted me and took off for the scrub. I chased them at a gallop through the gidgee and mulga scrub until they went to ground under a thicket of turkey bush. Feeling cocky, I rode my horse in close to nudge the beasts onto their feet. They were having none of that, and stayed down until I was over the top of them trying to kick them into life. Just then, about half a ton of snorting meanness in the form of a wide eyed, horny red shorthorn cross cow came up with its horns under the belly of the horse I was riding and lifted both of us a full three feet (1 metre) off the ground. I was frantically driving my boot heel at its head, trying to

get the beast to back off, at the same time working to keep the horse on his feet. It would have been a long walk back if he'd been injured. There were many of these self-learned lessons. You never forget 'em, and they all added to the sum of your experience.

You work with some interesting characters. One moonlit night we were all in our swags when there was a thump and someone said, 'What was that?' 'Only a snake,' said an old stockman. A little while later, another thump. Same question, same reply. This was repeated at intervals and by morning there were eight tiny dead snakes lined up by the old boy's swag. He had just rolled over, grabbed his boot and smashed them with the heel.

Life went on like that – a bit of station work on those bullock depots down along the Cooper and the Barcoo, a couple of droving trips to the rail at Quilpie, or moving stock from one station to another. Then late one afternoon I found myself sitting on a stock horse, stockwhip crooked in my arm, battered old Akubra pulled low to shade my eyes as we slowly put the mob together for the night, and I realised that I wasn't enjoying myself anymore. I thought to myself, 'I need a change'.

When the cattle were delivered I signed off, collected my pay cheque and that phase of my life was over. I'd had a lot of fun and done a lot of things. I'd ridden some memorable horses, experienced a lot and met some unforgettable people. I had gained experience as a bushman and now it was time to try something else. There were other directions I wanted to go, so for me it was time to 'catch the rattler'. I was going back to where I had grown up, Preston.

It was a long trip home on the rattler, and very different from the first journey I had taken when I left Preston in search of adventure.

At last, back in my own territory, I put down my saddle and gear by the back door, gave a knock and walked in.

'Hello Mum, I'm home.'

'Oh! Hello son,' said mum, 'have you had lunch?'

Just like all mothers do, God bless them.

CHAPTER 2

Horse mad

I've always thanked my mother for having the foresight to see that I was born in the country.

It was in the early thirties, during the worst part of the great depression, that my parents decided to move out of Melbourne to Daylesford, Victoria, where my father took a job as a hard rock miner. We lived between Daylesford and Hepburn Springs — exactly which dwelling we occupied depended on the seasons.

In wintertime we occupied a weatherboard holiday house belonging to the most straight-laced Victorian couple you could ever have met, my grandparents Fred and May Hood. When summer came they'd rent this house to visitors from Melbourne who would come to 'take the waters' at nearby Hepburn mineral springs, and mum, dad, my brother Alan and I would have to move into a nearby miner's hut. The earth floor was made of termite mound rammed flat and polished with skimmed milk. It was like marble until a kid picked a hole in it with the fire poker, then there'd be a smack on the bum followed by some wailing.

I can only guess how tough it was when I made my appearance in 1934 but, in the Australian way, my mum coped. Maybe that shaped my future outlook ... whatever happens, you cope with it.

My dad had an indomitable spirit that we all seemed to inherit. He indeed was a mighty man who was always willing to help out somebody in need, anyone from a neighbour to a down and out stranger. I was very young, but I'm sure I would have been proud to see him playing the big brass horn in the Miners' band, or playing the piano in the local hall.

Then he decided to dig a gold mine in the back yard. Whenever his pick and shovel struck hard rock he would descend, drill, and pack a charge. When all was right he'd light the fuse and get out, sometimes it seemed with undue haste. He would chop firewood from the bush and use a slice of gelignite to start the kitchen fire.

He'd tell us stories, fables or truths like the story of the lost 'Billycan reef', about the old prospector who finally found a rich reef in an almost hidden creek. The old boy marked the spot by hanging a billycan on a tree branch at the site and went away to register the claim, but when he returned he couldn't find the tree, the reef — or even the billycan.

Things weren't easy on the goldfields. We'd be listening to dad talking about his backyard mine and, with a wry grin on his face, he would say philosophically, 'Working underground you've gotta consider the cost, and if the money is getting a bit short, then the fuses will get even shorter.' I guess that accounted for the seeming 'undue haste'. But we coped, and somehow things just seemed to always work out.

The miners of the district had various ways to supplement their meagre income. When working in the mine, if they loaded a particularly rich skip of ore, the miner who loaded it might place a piece of wood on the rim of the skip. The pusher would tip the contents down a certain known side of the mullock heap, the idea being that in the future they could ferret around and find that ore, crush it, separate it and sell the gold.

Another more open lot were the 'spotters', those eagle-eyed men who would go out after rain with a glass jar in hand and walk the dirt tracks and gutters of the district. If their keen eyes spotted a tiny speck of the precious metal they would lick their fingertip, touch the speck and drop it into the glass jar. With gold, if you think it's gold, it is gold. If you are not sure, you can be sure it isn't gold.

There were always the fossickers. At any time these men would be gouging creek banks, gutters and rock crevices looking for colour, then with a pan they'd wash their pay dirt in the creek to reveal the gold. After rain Dad would sweep down the gravel paths around the house and pan the sweepings. Even the slightest colour could buy enough to make a meal.

The depression finally ground to a finish and dad found work in Melbourne. They say 'You can take the boy out of the bush, but you can't take the bush out of the boy'— although I was very young when we left Daylesford, the bush never left me.

Everything in North Fitzroy was new to me. I'd been used to a dirt road, a creek and a gold shaft behind the house. Now, for the first time I was living with other kids next door and a kid named Tom over the lane. Dad had built my brother a billycart out of a fruit box, the sort that had iron wheels and rope reins, and my brother would drag me all over the suburb, up lanes and through parks. It was while we were living in Fitzroy that our family was completed with the arrival of a delightful little sister, Valerie. We've been pals ever since.

My dad had a motorcycle, the sort you are always tinkering with. It was an Indian. Being complete with a sidecar, it certainly was not the world's fastest Indian, but we'd have wonderful day trips in it. There'd be Dad in his leather coat, helmet and goggles at the controls, big brother proudly riding pillion, and me perched on the fuel tank covering unimportant items like the fuel gauge and the speedometer. Mum rode in the sidecar nursing Val, wrapped cocoon-like in her satin-edged blanket. They are warm and happy memories.

Things must have been looking up for we moved again, this time to a rented house in Preston. In those days Preston was the outermost suburb in that area of Melbourne. The weatherboard house was big and only one block from my first school; I could start running on the first bell and never be late. There were hundreds of kids in the district, and the big nearly-new Preston East State School was crowded, with upwards of sixty kids in a class and only one teacher per class. We didn't expect anything different. That's how it was, but we were taught. We learned to read and write very early in our school life. I'd say I had a very good start to my schooling. I learned fast, I learned well and through the year I advanced to the first grade.

When World War II broke out my dad immediately joined the army (A.I.F, Sixth Division). I vividly recall the day he walked into the kitchen and, with a silly grin, said to mum, 'I've joined up'. Dad ducked when mum hit the roof and let loose with a couple of teacups. We had all been through hard times, and mum didn't need this.

On my sixth birthday dad sailed off to the Middle East leaving mum, three kids and very little money. We kids tried to help and to accept things as they were. We understood not to be a bother and to ask for nothing. I realised that I was a big kid now I was six, and I'd have to learn to stand on my own two feet

Then I found I could draw. In my early years at school I was drawing fighter planes, Spitfires and Hawker Hurricanes, on the other kids' schoolbooks. After Pearl Harbour I'd draw American fighters; planes like the Mustang and the twin fuselage Lockheed Lightning. As my schooling progressed, in lieu of arithmetic I was asked to do illustrations of all the nature study items. These ranged from grasshoppers, case moths and stick insects, to plant life of all sorts. Although blank paper was scarce, my mother encouraged my drawing and saved every bit she could for me. In later life this gift would be a great asset, particularly in leather carving. Every bit of tooling I did was drawn freehand directly onto the leather.

In the early part of the war council workers came to the schoolyard and dug deep zigzag slit trenches in the hard clay soil of the play areas. Once these trenches were finished we would have 'air raid drill'. We'd be sitting in our classrooms and someone would ring the assembly bell. 'Air raid drill,' the teacher would say, and we would march to the trenches and sit fidgeting until the all clear was sounded.

Big brothers seemed to know all the answers, so I asked Alan, 'Why are the trenches zigzagged?' He replied, 'When the Jap planes dive down to machine gun you, they only get the kids in the middle, they don't get the ones in the points.' Big brothers were always ready to give bits of information as useful as this. The talk of being machine-gunned didn't bother us, except that, from then on, each air raid drill we who were in the know would always sit in the pointy bits. We knew which side was up.

During the early part of the war, when dad was in the Libyan Desert or somewhere like that, we moved to another house up the street. In the front garden mum dug flowerbeds, I'm sure she got comfort from growing flowers. But without a man in the house we didn't have the luxury of a vegetable garden. The large quarter-acre back yard of the house we lived in was totally feral, a perfect place for kids to get lost in their fantasies. Other kids would come to our place and be cowboys, Indians, pirates, gangsters or they'd play the parts of the 'Our Gang' movies. Their own fathers had gardens in their yards and they weren't allowed to play there so they played in ours. We'd build forts and we'd scrape out depressions and call them air raid shelters. My gold mine was producing chunks of sandy quartz, but rain put an end to my endeavours when the mine filled with water.

The war gave us kids freedom. When we weren't playing in the back yard we'd spend our time roaming the streets or the paddocks. The older we got, the further we'd roam, and that was OK as long as we were back before it got too dark. We'd do just what we wanted, and if that upset a grown-up… we'd get a clip over the ears. We weren't 'brought up'; with no help we 'growed' like weeds, no special treatment, just a safe home and good friends.

Kids like us never went into somebody else's house, we'd stand at the gate calling out, 'Biiiilly!' until that kid came out. Or if he couldn't get out we'd go to another kid's house and call out his name. It was a great time to be a kid. As far as grown-ups went we didn't exist, so we did our own thing.

One afternoon when I was about eight I was helping my big brother build a billycart; in those days we called them 'trucks'. In the construction phase of the truck Alan made the request, 'Grab some nails from the big box in there' and, always willing, I raced, grabbed a goodly handful, and fell arse over head as I bolted out through the shed doorway. Regaining my feet, I looked down to check for damage and saw a rusty three-inch nail sticking right through the palm of my right hand…in one side and out the other.

Big brothers are always there to help, so he walked me out to the street and attracted the attention of the bread cart driver. The driver lifted me into the cart, gave the horse a click of the tongue and drove us to the local medico. Dr Lear just hauled the nail out, gave me a tetanus shot, dabbed on a bit of Mercurochrome and home I went. No tears, no nothing. When the billycart was finished Alan would drag it and me to the shopping strip, we'd get the groceries or half a hundredweight of firewood then, with me on top and at the risk a wreck, he'd race back home at top speed.

Although we were on the edge of the city, it was like living in the country. The main stock route from the grazing country up north ran down to Gippsland through the paddocks just a few streets from us. There was a big drought in nineteen forty something and I remember seeing the paddocks entirely covered by thousands of head of sheep. They were in full wool and were being walked down to Gippsland for the good grass.

I hadn't seen Dad for a long time but that was all right, he was a soldier and he was my hero. Then one afternoon I was perched high on the gable of the house when I looked down and saw my dad, in uniform with his full army kit, walking through the front gate. I scurried along the roof and as I was climbing down the awning I felt his comforting hands as, with a big grin, he lifted me to the ground. I was so pleased to see him. I followed him inside to see mum and sis. Then like a boy, I donned his tin hat and gas mask, grabbed his rifle and disappeared down the backyard to the fort we had scraped out in the big patch of red geraniums. I was watching out for the enemy. I couldn't wait to be a real soldier.

I sure wished I was a real soldier one day when I came home from school and found mum and her sister, my Auntie Irene, very upset. It was during the worst part of the war, my dad was away fighting, and I guess there wasn't enough money to pay the meagre gas bill. The meter reader had threatened to cut off the gas, and when I heard this it made me hopping mad. We were without a father to help, and here he was threatening my mum. I was only about eight, but I wanted to kick his shins and punch his face in. I think maybe the neighbour across the road might have helped with the few bob needed.

Occasionally in the school holidays mum would take us by train back to Daylesford. Those old steam trains were memorable, straight out of the Victorian era. You never forget the sting of a lump of coal soot the size of a brick in your eye, and the faces you'd pull as mum dug it out with the corner of her handkerchief. And it seems that on every trip the train would not make it up the big hill on the first run and we'd have to back up for miles to give it another try. It could take up to three attempts before some heavy puffing finally got us over the top and we'd make the run to Daylesford.

I was eleven or twelve when my Dad came home from the war, and I recall that we kids spent a week with our grandparents. I guess mum and dad had things to do that week. I'm sure he came home with no hang-ups. He just took a job, bought the house we lived in, and continued raising us kids. It was so good to have a father in the house. For the last five years my older brother Alan and a school friend, John Miller, had been regular steadying influences, someone solid on whom I could rely.

My life started to change when I graduated to Tech School. I was a teenager; I was beginning to grow up. When I first went to Tech school I'd draw motorcycles, but I pretty soon changed to horses. If I couldn't have one, I'd draw them. My ideas came from illustrations in cowboy books and comics.

With guidance from my father, who was a carpenter and joiner, and by learning the skill at school, I became very proficient at woodwork. I got high marks for technical drawing and sheet metal work, drawing just came naturally, I also liked English Grammar but I was not so keen on Maths. I did like the idea that everything is run on mathematical principles, but my teachers didn't seem to have the patience to teach any kid less than the brightest and smartest. Many teachers were returned soldiers, who seemed to be shell-shocked or to have some other form of mental disorder. I was too young to realise that the war had permanently scarred their lives.

I left school as soon as the law would allow and took an apprenticeship as an engineering patternmaker, a trade which would utilise all those class skills in which I was competent. From then on I was earning money, and I saved hard to buy the thing I wanted most.

Five to ten quid ($10-20) would buy a horse.

I named him Long Tom, after Daniel Boone's Kentucky rifle. He was an old cavalry remount, lean and tall, but he was quiet and he'd carry three of us at a lope. The main thing was that he was mine.

Like all army remounts, Tom's brand showed the year
he was foaled (early 1940s). He was totally reliable, game,
easy to shoe, and he would go anywhere; a good first horse.
I didn't have him long, but I learned many important basics
from him. After Tom, I knew how to pick a good looking,
sound, strong, and willing horse more suited to my size, and
from that point on the fun never stopped. Neither did the
search for adventure.

I rode big Tom so much that he needed shoes. I had worn
his feet away and it was time to take him to a blacksmith's
shop to get him shod. I knew where to take him, the forge
of Mr Dawes in St George's Road, Northcote. Years earlier,
on visits to our grandparents, my sister and I would sit inside
the door of the forge and watch, fascinated by the ring of the
anvil and the glow of the red-hot metal as the shoes were
being forged. It seemed natural for me to ride to that same
shop for Tom's first set of shoes.

The farrier told me what he was doing as he shaped
the horse's feet, fitted them, and nailed the shoes on. I was
intrigued when I saw that the nails he used were in an old felt
hat on the floor at his feet, and asked him about it. 'This way
it don't rattle, they don't spill out and a horse can't knock 'em
over,' he explained.

Eight weeks later, when those shoes had worn and rattled
loose, I was back again for another set. After a while I figured
I could save money by shoeing old Tom myself. The shoes still
had plenty of wear so I decided to re-use them. With a pair
of pinchers and one of my dad's claw hammers I removed the
shoes. I had bought a box of nails so, remembering what I'd
learned, I got stuck into it and nailed the shoes back on …
only just. The next time I shod him I poured the nails from
the box into an old army slouch hat I had, and that's the way
I did it from then on.

Horses … there were plenty about when we grew up.
Farmers were going mechanical and were giving up on

horses. Every small farm in the district would have a few in a paddock somewhere on the place. You'd approach the farmer to see if he wanted to sell, he'd 'um', and 'ah,' think about it for a while and tell you he was probably 'gunna use 'em on the place'. You'd turn to go, he'd call you back, think about it again, then finally relent and sell you one… but we'd inevitably had to go through this dickering ritual. Those horses we bought were cheap, but they were a totally unknown quantity. They'd be anything from fair in harness or under saddle to being fat and lazy, or completely useless. Quite often they'd be unbroken, ill mannered and downright dangerous. But we bought them and if they were no bloody good we just sold them on again.

Every weekend in the want ads of the newspapers there'd be a half-page of horses for sale. Always present were the horse dealers like Arthur Peddie of Clifton Hill, Victor Venn from West Heidelberg, Eric Lawrence and the renowned Bluey

Diamond. Added to that, there were hundreds of private sales, usually from fathers who just wanted to get rid of the horse their daughter had fallen in love with not a year before but had since discovered boys. Or maybe she just found out that she couldn't ride anyway.

As horse kids we'd spend a lot of our weekends with Bluey Diamond and Lofty Cannard at Bluey's place. Later we would be working with that indefatigable pair of horse traders. They would travel the country buying unwanted horses from cattle and sheep stations in New South Wales, Queensland and as far away as the Birdsville track in

South Australia and walk them for many hundreds of miles to the outskirts of Melbourne. There, anything that looked like it could be ridden was drafted off and trucked or walked to a big paddock just out of Rosanna and run into a high bush pole yard for the weekend. They'd be advertised for sale in the Saturday newspapers as riding hacks and we young kids were the test pilots.

There's nothing like your mates watching from the fence and the hard ground of a horse yard to make you want to stay in the saddle, no matter how hard the horse bucks. Then if you did part company you wouldn't just land with a thud, it would be a spectacular wreck that would be talked about for weeks to come.

Army remounts (Long Tom's mob) were really obsolete by the late forties and were sold off to the public. Horses from all directions came through the popular horse auctions at Dandenong or Newmarket sale yards. Each lot would be ridden, led, or driven into the ring, and if you had already picked out something you liked, you'd wait for its lot number to turn up in the ring, then you'd bid. But like any auction of the time it was *caveat emptor*, 'Let the buyer beware'.

Of course there were all the racehorses that were too slow for the track, they had to go somewhere so most of them ended up being bought by girls for use as saddle hacks. If you wanted something to go in harness there were the equally slow square-gaited trotting horses or retired baker's cart and milk delivery horses. The prices for these horses were low mainly because the killer market was still small. The zoo always wanted aged or broken down horses to provide meat for the lions, but the pet food market was in its infancy.

I was always ready to trade a horse. Many of us would go out in the morning on one horse, see something we liked and do a deal; maybe we'd even swap horses. I always made sure I ended up with a good one, and if I rode home bareback I didn't mind; you could bet I'd done all right.

It was when we were going to school and learning about the Australian outback that we developed such a pride in being Australian. In those teenage years I wanted to become like Chips Rafferty, that tall lanky true Australian with the slow easy drawl and the great big grin. Some of us felt we just had to see and feel the great outback with no rush and no hurry, so for us travelling by horse was the natural thing to do. From then on my life went on an unswerving course of adventurous fun and learning, leading to the outback, the west and saddlemaking, and ultimately to be the best-known western saddlemaker in Australia.

As teenagers we started to form friendships. A group of us would meet at a friend's place most evenings after work. One kid I went to Tech school with said that his brother rode horses and that they lived over the creek in West Heidelberg. The next Saturday I rode over to say g'day The brother and I compared horses, talked horse stuff and saddle stuff, found we had a lot in common, and from then on we knocked about together. This was Neville Page, later to call himself Spinifex Mick, who would be my travelling companion when we went north looking for adventure.

From a very young age, before I ever owned a horse, I'd stand fascinated in his saddlery and watch Harry Jensen at work. He'd be sitting there in his waistcoat and apron, awl and needles in hand, sewing at lightning speed doing what looked to be a sleight of hand trick. His saddlery was in Plenty Road, Preston and we horse-mad kids visited him regularly. We'd watch as he repaired a saddle, his work held in a set of clamps; or he'd be making a bridle or a set of reins. We all became familiar with the pleasing smell of harness and saddle leather.

When I became well known as a saddlemaker Harry claimed with pride that he taught me how to hand sew, which was true. He also taught every kid in the district to hand sew, and he taught us well. Because of good old tradesmen like

Harry who were willing to pass on their skills, I was able to learn enough to repair gear that might get broken due to hard work or as the result of a wreck.

I also learned a lot from blacksmiths. Blacksmiths' shops were always warm and inviting, and on cold wet days there'd always be a few old codgers sitting around talking; they'd come in to get warm and they'd stay all day. In those days you'd ride to the blacksmith shop and the farrier would make the shoes, fit them hot and nail them on, so very soon a group of us would meet at the forge. There was always a chance for some hands-on work 'striking', where you swing a ten-pound sledgehammer while the blacksmith draws out steel. There were a few of us who wanted to learn to shoe properly; although I'd been shoeing my own horses, I knew I still had a lot to learn.

If we wanted to help and learn, the first job we'd be given would be to remove the old shoes and dress the horse's feet to prepare them for the new set. ('Aren't they called hooves?' someone asked me once. 'Well, the mighty Jack McLaren, the blacksmith who taught me so much, always called them feet,' I replied, 'and that's good enough for me'.) Jack's forge was in High Street, Preston and I spent a lot of time working there to help and to learn as much as I could. I was dedicated to the task, and it wasn't long before I was nailing on during the Saturday morning visits with our gang. Nailing on is no hit-and-miss affair, you only have about 6mm of thickness in which to drive the nails.

I'd strike for Mack as he made the shoes, and either Mack or I would hot fit them. A great teacher was Mack. One time when he had passed me a red-hot shoe to burn onto the hoof, I tried the shoe and found it to be twisted, so I put down the horse's foot and took the shoe to have him straighten it. Mack looked at it and said in his booming voice, 'If it's wrong, don't bring it over, throw it at me, it's my mistake'.

I enjoyed shoeing Preston Council's big dray horses.

These Clydesdales had feet the size of manhole covers. I'd be burning on a gigantic horseshoe; it wouldn't be just red hot, it'd be a yellow, almost welding heat. There's me under the horse, coughing and spluttering in a cloud of rancid yellow hoof smoke, and Mack's comment would be...'Stop moaning! You should be able to do the drawback on that.'

Or maybe I'd be nailing on, using a hat full of size twelve nails the size of pier spikes. I'd be driving the nails in, tap, tap, hit, hit, hit and finally Mack would turn around with a grin and roar, 'Three hits with that, you're not playing the bloody piano'. And that made me more diligent. There were other times when we'd be shoeing a hack, I'd be nailing on a front shoe and I'd feel the horse lurch a little. I'd look back and there'd be Mack with a hind leg off the ground fitting a hot shoe. That's the way to learn – I'd be nailing on at the front end and at the same time Mack would be behind me, shoeing the half that was sticking out the back.

Mack taught so many of us so much, a lot of the kids became full time horse shoers. But apart from shoeing horses, he was a great storyteller. I'm certain the stories were all true because they never varied. Mack had been a Farrier Sergeant with the Australian Army in the Middle East during the First World War. Just like the vets, the farriers were responsible for thousands of horses; the vets tended bullet wounds and the farriers kept the horses' feet shod and in good order.

One winter afternoon I was helping Mack to dress a heap of the local council's picks and crow-bars; Jack was on the anvil and I was striking. As we worked he told the story of the time in Egypt when his troop was riding past a shelled railway station. Through the open door, in the rubble Mack spotted a large iron safe. Figuring something should be done about it, he and a few of his mates got together and hired a taxi. They threw in a portable forge, an anvil, a bag of coke, some hand hammers, cold chisels and a sledgehammer. Then they all piled in on top and drove to the station and the safe.

The forge was lit, the coke was piled on and soon the fire was roaring. While that was going on the other boys were attacking the safe with cold chisels ... bash, bash ... until the chisels were dull. As soon as a chisel lost its edge, it was thrown to Mack on the forge, where he'd dress it, sharpen and harden it. Mack went on with the tale. They worked long into the evening, two men chiselling, another man striking and Mack on the anvil sharpening and hardening the tools, until they finally broke through

Mack stopped working for just a moment and, with a distant look in his eye he said, 'Y' know, after all that, the bloody safe was empty.'

There were always a few young helpers who were willing to learn to work on the anvil. In a jobbing shop you take on any work that comes along, from making wrecking bars to dressing the council picks. One very impressive job was drawing out and dressing excavator tines. These were super tough and four inches square, drawn down to a chisel point. When they wore out and lost their cutting edge it was up to the blacksmith to draw out and reform the points. That's where we came in. Mack would bring these great lumps of steel to brilliant glowing yellow heat and, supporting it with a chain, he would swing it to the anvil. Three of us with fourteen-pound sledgehammers would swing in unison and, guided by Mack with his hand hammer, we'd work that steel down. We would draw out these massive things and feel good when they were all done.

It's funny how one simple event can be life-changing. In the early 1950s I was going to trade school in Melbourne and one lunch time I took a walk to Morrison's saddle shop in Bourke Street. There I bought that Australian icon, a stockwhip. It was eight feet (2.4 m) of twelve-plaited kangaroo, with a plaited handle, a red hide tail, and on the end I fitted a horsehair cracker. After wrapping it around my neck a few times it wasn't long before I'd got a few cracks out of it and soon I figured I was a pretty good whip cracker.

There wasn't a flower in mum's garden that was safe; I'd ride around on my saddle horse going crack, crack, bloody crack at every opportunity. This continued until I cracked the tail of the whip down to the plaiting. Then somebody said, 'There's a bloke living down in Thornbury, he'll fix it for you.'

I was directed to the backyard workshop of John Chirnside, who turned out to be the finest leather worker I have ever known.

After spending a couple of hours talking and looking at the beautiful leather carving and the stockwhips he had made, he showed me the first western saddle I ever saw. He'd built the saddle on a tree he had formed with great difficulty, and that fired my interest.

It was time for me to mount my horse and go. As I was leaving I asked, 'Will you fix my whip for me?' When John replied, 'No!' my spirits dropped and I asked him, 'Why not?' His reply was, 'You can fix it next time you're here.' I went back the next night and learned how to fix my whip.

I took such an interest in John's beautiful leatherwork that I started to learn. I learned very simple things to start off with, but this finally led to very complex leatherwork and finally to saddlery.

How did I get around to taking on such a task? I had never seen an American saddle, either being ridden in or even abandoned in a barn. It was just by 'happenstance' that in John Chirnside's workshop was that replica roping saddle that he'd laboriously built. I expressed a great interest in it, and after a while he said to me, 'Put it on your horse and go for a ride.' There was no holding me back. I saddled up and I swung on board. I seemed to just slide into it; the saddle fitted me like a glove. I went for a ride and when I returned I didn't want to get out of it. I said to Chirny, 'Why don't you make more saddles like this, it's great.' His response was, 'I would, but I can't get trees, it's illegal to import them, and nobody I know could make one'.

'What do they look like?' I asked, and John took an American saddle catalogue from a shelf in his workshop. The catalogue was of Hamley & Co, Pendleton Oregon, reputedly America's finest saddle and tree makers.

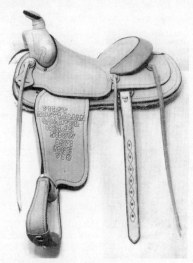

'See that,' said John, 'how they carve the tree out of wood and cover it with rawhide?' He went on, 'I couldn't make one and I haven't found anybody who could'. That's where my youthful cockiness came to the fore. The structure of the saddletree didn't worry me at all. I looked at the picture, glanced at John and said, 'I reckon I could.'

My training as an engineering patternmaker, a highly skilled woodworking trade, was coming to the fore. A patternmaker's job is to make the most complex wooden forms, the patterns, which are then used in a foundry in the production of castings in iron, bronze, aluminium, steel or any other metal. The skill lay in not only being able to work with wood, but having the ability to envision the finished article from a blueprint, a drawing or even a photograph. I wanted to give it a try.

John understood this and replied, 'Well, make two, and we'll make a saddle each'. That's how my interest in western got started. I'd finished my apprenticeship and was working in a small pattern shop in Preston. My boss gave me a billet of spruce and I used the shop bandsaw to shape the components.

That saddle I was building for myself was an American-style roping saddle (see illustration page 43). A western saddle has a standing part in front called the fork, and a cantle to form the seat. Fixed to the forepart or fork is the saddle horn. This horn has many uses – originally used for roping and catching cattle on the open range, it is handy when mounting an unruly horse or for ponying a young colt. Ponying is training a youngster to get used to the lead by dallying the colt's lead around the saddle horn so that he will walk beside your horse. The colt can do what it likes, the lead won't slip, and a good horse will ignore the youngster. An hour or two beside a good steady horse and the colt will be very agreeable.

For the tree I designed and glued the fork and cantle; the fork was laminated for strength and carved to shape. The trees are built using two bars; these are the parts that come in contact with the horse. Onto these bars are fitted the fork and the cantle. The wooden cantle is made to form a seat and carefully shaped to fit the rider's rear end.

Once I had the trees formed for those first two saddles, I took them and a spokeshave to several horses and worked until I had achieved a good comfortable surface on their backs. To this wooden tree is fitted a bronze casting in the form of the saddle-horn. To make the horns, I carved the shape from wood and took this pattern to a foundry. The foundry men used the horn pattern to make a sand mould, into which molten bronze was poured. I picked up the castings, drilled them and let them into the forepart or 'fork' of the wooden tree.

I had made those two trees in the workshop at home, and one Saturday I took them to Chirny's workshop, where the two of us laboriously covered and laced them with rawhide to give them strength. Rawhide is the hide of a cow or steer once the hair and excess fat has been removed in a lime bath and the lime has been washed out. The rawhide is laced onto the tree while it is wet, and it tightens as it dries. The saddletree will then have the strength to hold a thousand pound beast. That's what I was told, and I've proved it right a hundred times.

Starting this saddle was to have a profound effect on the rest of my life. John Chirnside, master leather craftsman, guitar player and horseman was to become my teacher, lifetime friend and mentor. My father had always said to me, 'Knowledge is no burden to carry' and, as an adjunct to that, he also said, 'Listen and look when you are being shown something, don't interrupt and say you know. Could be something there you don't know'.

So I looked, I listened and I learned.

1950s Australian
stock saddle

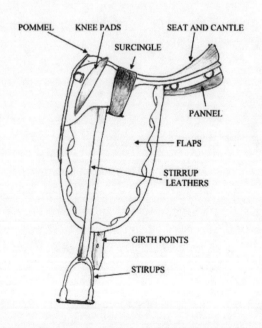

1950s 'Bob Crosby' calf roping saddle

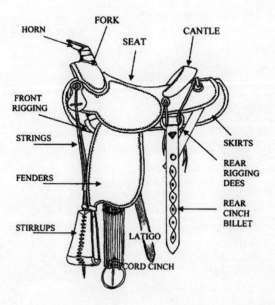

HORN

FORK

SEAT

CANTLE

FRONT RIGGING

STRINGS

FENDERS

STIRRUPS

SKIRTS

REAR RIGGING DEES

REAR CINCH BILLET

LATIGO

CORD CINCH

CHAPTER 3

'Let's go bush'

Most of us had left school and were working by the time we reached fifteen. We had money; not a lot, but then again we didn't need a lot. Before long we had become a fair sized mob of young, game, horse-mad kids. We knocked around together on horses of all types, from good-looking saddle horses to tough, ordinary-looking hacks of doubtful lineage. Usually there would be a few girls riding with us, and they all rode incredibly tall thoroughbreds. I'd be there on my fourteen-and-a-half or fifteen-hand saddle horse looking up to talk to a younger girl towering over me on a well groomed and well presented seventeen-hand giant, usually chestnut. Every suburb seemed to have at least one big crowd of kids of mixed gender, mostly teenagers, who rode around together. Other kids would join in and others would peel off to do their own thing. There was seldom any trouble; we were just wild and free, as all kids should be.

Not all of the kids I went to school with took to horses; some drove cars. Drive-ins were new, and if a kid had a car we'd all pile in and off we'd go. If it was a cowboy picture, just a heap of guys would go. But if it was a romantic movie, we'd take girls for company.

Preston was the place where the city ended and the paddocks started. Within earshot of where I grew up was Tierney's dairy farm. They also grazed their cattle on the adjoining unfenced abandoned farmland we all knew as Healy's paddock. Every kid should have access to a place like Tierney's. We'd muck around and learn to handle stock, which was to prove useful to some of us in later years. We would push the cows up for milking, and we'd have rodeos riding the poddy calves. As well, we learned to avoid being confronted by the resident bull. We also learned to drive the mighty red roan delivery mare, and to use the flatbed lorry to feed out hay for the cattle.

Most of our weekends we just mucked around with our horses. There would be maybe a half a dozen to twenty or so who'd knock around together. We all thought we were pretty cool.

Very few kids in my time grew up in a horsey family. The farm kids around mostly had a disdain of horses; they certainly knew nothing about them. I took to horses purely for my own reason. I wanted to live the Australian dream, and owning a horse was something we just did.

Without knowledge or experience, we learned as we went. When I bought Tom, all I had with me was a length of rope. I paid the few quid for the horse and used the rope to ride him home. When I did get him home I wondered what the hell I was going to do with this giant animal now that I owned him. So I just tethered him with the same lump of rope, figuring I'd soon learn. There was always somebody around who would show you what to do. One afternoon I was leading my horse home from the paddocks when an old codger stopped me and said, 'I'll show you the knot to tie around a horse's neck, it will never slip and you can always untie it.' I listened intently, and as he showed me he told me his job was to tie scaffolding. The knot he showed me was a bowline, the main horseman's knot. I've used that knot ever since, and I haven't forgotten the old gent who showed me how to tie it.

We'd teach ourselves to ride with a rope over the horse's nose or, if he was a bit flighty, through his mouth. That way we could go for a ride at any time, just by slipping on a rope and cantering off bareback. It didn't take long before we graduated to bridles and then saddles, and with these we became pretty competent on the back of a horse. Maybe we weren't great horsemen, but we were game and nothing daunted us. We'd go anywhere and do anything, and no matter what horse I was riding, he was for sale ... at a price.

Life was certainly simple for us kids at that time, and we all had a dream. We had been taught about the exploits of the explorers, we had read of Banjo Patterson and Henry Lawson, we had heard stories of the great sheep and cattle stations, and many of us took to the Australian way. We wanted to relive the stories of 'Clancy of the Overflow'. All we needed was a riding horse under us to live the dream. We rode the endless paddocks that surrounded us; there were very few laws, and very little traffic, and being surrounded by other kids with their horses added to the fun. 'Going bush' seemed a natural thing for us to do.

Every now and then Neville and I would get an urge to drive a vehicle. One of those times, Neville had a vehicle and I had a good-looking black Galloway mare called Sox. She was a fair sort of riding horse, except for a propensity to bolt. This wasn't so bad under saddle, but not good at all when you were riding bareback. When she was in harness, whoever was driving would have a good grip on the reins, the vehicles we drove were so light that there would be little if any strain on the traces. But Sox'd be happy going at her own chosen speed, usually flat out.

Neville had found an old piano box buggy and he'd cut it down to the barest essentials. All that was left were the four wheels, shafts and a tray, no dash, no brakes and he'd removed the seat. We harnessed Sox and decided to take a pleasant drive towards Greensborough. The two of us were sitting on this flimsy, narrow wooden platform and the little lady was fairly flying. We felt like we were in a scene from a John Ford western as grey rooster tails of dirt were thrown up from the wheels as we navigated the sweeping curves of the narrow winding dirt tracks in the open bushland at the back of Bundoora. Over his shoulder Neville said 'I saw a heavy buggy at Vic's place and it's got brakes 'n everything. We'll borrow it…that should slow the mare down.'

We drove to West Heidelberg at breakneck speed and in cloud of dust hauled the mare to a stop in the horse yards behind the St Hellier Street house. Vic's buggy was quite posh, with its flashy paint job, deep upholstered seats, side lamps, brakes and folded down hood. Sox was on her best behaviour as she jogged sedately down the drive and, with a gentle application of the brakes, we turned onto the roadway. All was going nicely as we trotted smartly along the road, acknowledging the admiring looks we got from the onlookers.

Just for style, and to catch a bit of shade, we decided to raise the hood. One of us applied the side lever and the hood raised, but it didn't stop where it should have, it went straight over us and landed over the mare's unsuspecting rump. Flighty at the best of times, Sox didn't take kindly to this indignity. With a high-pitched squeal she promptly dropped her head and started to buck and kick. When she finally stopped bucking the buggy was in a hundred pieces, which Neville and I gathered and tipped onto a nearby vacant lot. With all that done, and in lieu of payment, we left the buckboard at Vic's place. After that, with Sox still draped in what was left of the harness, we mounted and rode her double back to Neville's place. I don't know if these things that happened were 'experiences' or just a sort of 'school of hard knocks'.

One Saturday night Neville called on me to help move a good classy vehicle between suburbs. It was a jinker; a high two-wheeled single horse sulky, and we were to deliver it to somebody in Thornbury, a suburb closer to the city. We didn't want to bring a horse and harness to drive the thing there, so we decided to deliver it using Nev's BSA Bantam two-stroke motorcycle. We backed the bike between the shafts and set off, with Neville as pilot and me riding on the parcel rack holding a shaft in each hand. We were doing all right in the quiet side streets, but things were knocked out of whack when we reached Plenty Road, Preston, a major thoroughfare complete with tram tracks.

Trouble started when the narrow wheels of the jinker got stuck in the tram tracks, which started to dictate where we were going and, regardless of our intentions, the tracks took us around a corner in front of a picture theatre. We were holding our own until we caught up with a tram stopped in front of us. Neville applied the brakes on the bike but I couldn't hold the jinker back or steer it off the track; Inertia then took over and carried it and us along, straight into the back of the tram.

No one was hurt, no damage done, but the tram passengers were somewhat inconvenienced. After alighting from the tram they had to walk around the jinker and the fallen motorcycle, then step over our two bodies, in order to get to the picture theatre on the opposite side of the road. The tram went on its way, we regrouped and continued, this time straight ahead and away from the tram track. Nothing broken, nothing lost.

My grandad had a story about a sulky. He and his girlfriend hired a horse and sulky to go on a picnic. They tied the horse to a fence, but after a while they felt sorry for the horse just standing there all afternoon, so they decided to take it out of harness. Inexperienced in the ways of harness, they undid every buckle, piece by piece, but when they wanted to drive home they couldn't put it back together again. I don't remember the outcome, but the mishap didn't ruin the romance. Grandad's girlfriend finished up being my dear old grandmother.

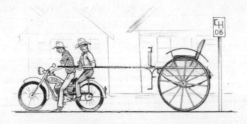

It was a Saturday afternoon in 1954, and a crowd of us were sitting around on our horses wondering what to do and where to go. Suddenly Neville Page, the coolest of us all, had an epiphany and spoke three words that led to a great adventure. Out of the blue came a nonchalant, 'Let's go bush'.

Those simple words rang pretty clear to me, but one kid, not noted for his quick grasp of reality, said 'What d'you mean?'

'We could buy a little wagon, take our horses and head bloody north', Nev replied.

'What'll we do when we get there?' asked the same kid.

'Go mustering, droving, drinking, chasing girls and horse breaking,' Nev and I said as one.

'Not for me,' was the retort from the same kid, 'too far from the Saturday night dance'.

'Go to your stupid dance, do what you bloody like', we said, 'we're going'.

From then on Neville and I and a couple of others hatched our plan.

Everything came to a halt for a few months when a call up notice to do my deferred national service turned up. I'd hoped I could have avoided it for a while, figuring if they couldn't find me then they couldn't catch me, but I got sprung. Nothing wrong with that, it just held us up a bit. Just a few months living in a tent at Puckapunyal, a big army camp in north-east Victoria. Army life was all right, we were well fed, we had no responsibilities, all we had to do was rifle drill, shoot at things and guard other things, do long forced marches and blow things up. It was fun, but I was looking forward to getting back on a horse. I was looking forward to seeing Big Neville again, too, and getting on with the plans for our trip.

We knew we would have no trouble buying an old bread cart and a couple of good reliable harness horses. Harness we had…we might have sold or wrecked all the sulkies and buggies we'd owned, but we'd kept a few sets of good single harness.

I finished an apprenticeship to trade when I turned twenty, and worked around a while to earn some cash money (in those days we called it 'earning a quid'). Big Nev had bought another harness horse, so there was nothing to stop us now.

One day after work Neville called in and told me he had found just the thing. 'It's a little one-horse van, it's got motor wheels and will only cost us ten quid.'

'Sounds great', I replied, 'we'll pick it up next weekend'.

The next Saturday, after Nev had finished his bread round, we harnessed up a sturdy black light delivery horse I had recently bought. By the time we were ready to go he was fully rigged, complete with harness saddle, breeching, collar and traces draped all over him.

Nonchalantly the two of us rode right down Plenty Road, Preston, with me in front holding as much of the reins as I needed and Neville behind in charge of the bits of harness that were hanging down, like the traces and breeching as well as the remainder of the long driving reins, the fifteen feet I wasn't using.

It was a good thing we'd put winkers on him, so the horse wasn't able to look into the shop windows to see how ridiculous he looked, in full harness with two kids perched on top. So, carefree, he took us right down High Street, Northcote, ignoring double-decker buses as they passed us, belching great clouds of black smoke – even in those quieter years these were very busy roads – but nothing daunted us or the horse as we headed for Arthur Peddie's sale yard at Clifton Hill.

There it was, our wagon, little and green! Its motor wheels were twenty-three inches behind and twenty-one inches in front, which allowed for the turntable. We paid the price and went to the horse yard, where we backed the tough little guy into the shafts and hooked up the traces and the breeching. Neville took the reins, gave a click of the tongue and a light slap with the reins, and we proudly trotted back to Preston.

It hadn't taken long for the other kids to drop out, but Neville and I kept working on the wagon. We altered it a bit by fitting a false floor inside. We also put a tray between the axles, to carry heavy stuff and any horse feed we might have to buy. We figured we would store any spare harness, ropes, fire irons and stuff under the false floor and put our saddles, rifle, tucker, our swags and clothes on top. We would be able to sleep there too, if the weather turned really bad.

Now it was time to get those things we didn't have. We bought grey army blankets, cooking gear, an iron camp oven, a couple of billies, a fry pan, some tin plates, a tin opener, some eating irons and a couple of mugs, then some hurricane lamps and a gallon can of kerosene. Somehow we acquired a fire iron, that's a steel frame to put over the fire to support the pots and pans. Gelignite boxes made good tucker boxes.

Of course for drinking water we had to have a couple of the ubiquitous canvas water bags, obligatory for anyone travelling in the bush. Campers would have them hanging from a tree branch outside their tent, motorists in the bush would always have one strapped to the front bumper-bar.

Then we bought some bush gear for ourselves, including the popular R.M. Williams strap leg jeans and elastic-sided Cuban-heeled riding boots, plus that Australian essential, an Akubra hat. Everything we would need to be Australian stockmen

We already had all the horse gear we needed. We each had our own good old stock saddles, bridles, breastplate, crupper, saddle blankets, stock whips, saddlebags and quart pots.

We had harness for the wagon horses, but we still needed half a dozen pairs of good R.M. Williams chain hobbles and some tether rope. I also bought some collar check to use as saddle blankets to go either under a riding saddle or under a harness saddle. And in case any of us got an injury, we picked up a bottle of eurythmic hobble chafe, that good old blue wound paint for man or beast.

We stocked up with a few sets of Muir horseshoes; they weren't much good but I could shape them on an anvil and they'd do the job. I had all the shoeing gear we'd need.

'We got nails?' asked Big Neville.

'A whole hatful,' I replied.

'No foot, no horse,' the old saying goes, so the last job left to do before we hit the road was to shoe the harness horses. The saddle horses would be OK, they had shoes of sorts. We harnessed up and drove the wagon down to Wright's Bakery in Heidelberg. Neville had delivered for them and was allowed to use the forge in the old building, straight from the 1800s. I was on the hand hammer, Nev was striking, and on that Saturday afternoon the anvil rang as we shaped and fitted the horseshoes. Following in the footsteps of the great old tradesmen who taught us, we'd have no trouble keeping the horses' feet in good condition along the way.

We led the horses out of the dirt-floored forge to harness them to the wagon, and their brand new shoes clattered on the time-worn cobblestones as we crossed the yard. With Neville at the reins we proudly drove back to Nev's place, there in the open paddocks that were just starting to be referred to as 'Heidelberg Heights'. Then I rode back to spend my last night at home before our adventure began.

My parents weren't bothered at all where we went. They knew I had some sense, and this was a perfectly safe country. All Mum said was to make sure I didn't get some girl into trouble, and not to drink too much. Dad was happy that I'd finished my apprenticeship, saying as usual, 'You'll always have something to fall back on'.

Early next morning, after a hug and a quick goodbye to mum, I mounted my saddle horse and smartly cantered the open paddocks to Nev's place in West Heidelberg. We loaded our gear, harnessed up, tied our spare horses to the back and the shafts and said goodbye to Nev's dear mother, Sal.

Then, with a click of the tongue and a slap with the reins, we were on our way.

CHAPTER 4

The Long Paddock

By the time we left it was about May 1955. We took it easy for the first few days to let the horses settle in. Not far along the way was the Plenty gorge, a deep and winding canyon-like stretch of rugged bushland cut deep by the small but ebullient Plenty River. I had worked there for a short time with a couple of farmers, so we decided to stay the night at the farm. We easily navigated the wagon down the winding narrow track to the homestead, where we talked for a while about our trip, had dinner, and soon settled down for the night. The next morning we put the other workhorse in harness, thanked our hosts for the meals and were again on our way – or at least we thought we were.

Half way up the same very steep track we had driven down the night before, the new horse chucked in the towel and started jumping in and out of the collar. Then, ignoring a couple of slaps on the rump with the reins and a swipe with the whip, he started to back down again. The wagon jack-knifed and it looked like we would all finish at the bottom of the gorge. With a bit of quick thinking, one of us grabbed the horse's head and the other put a rock behind the wheel, so we were safe … but that useless hay burner was headed for the knackery. We phoned a truck driver friend, and took the dud horse to a knackery at Wattle Glen in the hills not far away, a place that belonged to the same horse trader who had sold him to big Neville not long before. When we got there the place was deserted, so we swapped that horse for a solid delivery type chestnut gelding that looked like a good willing worker.

We harnessed the new horse, put him in the shafts, and Nev took the driver's seat. A click of the tongue, the creak of harness leather as Big Red leaned into the collar, and we were bowling smartly along the narrow bitumen road that skirts the foothills. That night we camped on a grassy patch of open land near Wallan. In times gone by this was the 'common' – it was grazing land where the local townsfolk could run their milking cows, or a place where travellers could hold their livestock. Our horses had worked well, they were content, they'd been watered and there was lush, plentiful grass for them. We spent a comfortable night sleeping by the campfire.

With the big strong chestnut back in the shafts and big tall Neville driving the wagon, I saddled my riding horse to give him some work and to enjoy the feeling of sitting astride and riding free and easy. Sydney Road was the main trunk road between Melbourne and Sydney but in those days it was just a narrow strip of tough but low quality bitumen snaking through and followed the contours of the foothills of the Great Dividing Range. It seemed to be following the original wagon tracks of the pioneers. As long as we kept the horses well shod we were able to drive along the gravel edges, and that kept us out of the way of the semi-trailers and other road users. Car drivers would honk their horns and truck drivers would give us a blast of their hooters as they passed us.

As the road nears the gap of the dividing range you come to Pretty Sally, the long slow climb that winds around the sides of the hills. My horse was trotting smartly along the roadside and I was lost in the moment when suddenly Neville hollered, 'Me hat's blowed off!'

There it was, bowling along like a hoop on a wheel; a strong cross draft had taken it and it wasn't going to stop. Digging in the spurs I took chase, caught up with it, reached down at full gallop and picked it up just before it went over the edge to be lost in parts unknown. I cantered back and handed it to Nev.

'Thanks,' he said, 'nearly lost the bloody thing …think we oughter stop at the top of the hill and give the horses rest?'

'Yep!' I agreed, 'and give us a break too'.

There were plenty of reasons why Big Neville didn't want to lose his hat. Not only had he just bought it, but a hat was to be an essential part of our lives. A broad-brimmed hat will shade your eyes when riding into the sun, and keep the rain off your head in the wet. It'll protect your head if you hit a tree branch at speed, or you can fan a fire into life with it. You can use it to give a thirsty horse a drink, or to slap some manners into an unruly horse. And it's a handy repository for nails when you are shoeing a horse…as I've done a hundred times. So it is for use, not just an ornament.

We'd left Sydney road and were about a week into our trip and heading towards Echuca when a car-load of friends from our stomping ground in Preston and Heidelberg showed up in John Henry's posh as-new 1949 Oldsmobile. We stopped for a talk and a bite to eat, then they said, 'We'll drive ahead, find a good place and make camp. Look for a sign on the road'.

We continued on our way in the wagon until we came across an arrow of stones in the middle of the road pointing to a stock reserve in the bush, where our mates were lazing around a great roaring campfire. Obviously only one other car had passed in the hour or so they'd been there, because only one stone in the arrow had been knocked out of place. There was not much traffic back then.

We camped out that night and had a good wild time of it. There was no booze, but they brought along a heap of food, plus John Chirnside and his guitar. We spent the night with plenty to eat, plenty of music, plenty of songs and a heap of jokes. The gang stayed a few hours in the morning, cleaned up the camp, and helped us load the wagon and harness the workhorse of the day. Then, with a whoop and a holler, we were on the road again. The same crowd was to turn up later on a station where big Neville and I were working.

At about this time we acquired an old battered and tarnished army bugle. I don't know where we got it from, maybe we bought it in some junk shop, but we had it and we had fun with it. The horses knew the sound and would prick their ears at the first few wailing blasts, then after a while they just ignored it.

We had most fun with it in cattle country. Whenever one of us gave a resounding solo, every cow, steer, calf and bull within earshot would come trotting up, with fixated eyes and cupped ears and they'd follow us along the fence until the paddock ended. Then in the next paddock another line of bellowing and bawling cattle would be following until they came to a cross fence. We'd give another blast and another mob would lift their heads, start bellowing and do the same thing.

In Victoria, where the roadsides were fenced, the bugle was OK because the cattle were confined, but once we'd crossed the border into N S W we were in unfenced country and things were different. We'd give a blast, and any cattle around would come trotting after the wagon and we'd finish up in a sea of bellowing cattle all wanting to get a look at this noisy intruder. We stopped blowing the bugle. We'd had enough of it anyway.

We became expert in choosing a place to camp, a place with good green feed and water where we could let the horses graze free. In the country, school yards were good and so were church yards. In the towns, we'd set up camp in the trucking yards or maybe the local show ground. We'd saddle a couple of horses, water and yard the others, and ride off to explore the town. Neither of us drank much then; we'd grab something to drink or just stock up on food, but we made sure we cruised the main street. There's nothing like the clatter of horses' feet to turn the head of a pretty girl.

We crossed the Murray River into New South Wales at the town of Moama and headed north to Deniliquin. We were taking the route now called 'The Long Paddock' and in Allan Nixon's book *The Outbackers* my input formed the basis of the first chapter. Spinifex and I were on our way, and the weather was getting warmer day by day.

The train line runs parallel with the road on the way to Deniliquin and the drivers would give us a friendly blast of the whistle as they passed us. Those old trains had a romance about them that I surely miss. That hollow huff the engine makes when they are sitting big and black at a station, boilers fired up, in a cloud of white steam ... the engineer oiling the sliding bits with his extremely long-spouted oil-can ... the unforgettable smell of steam and lubricating oil hanging on the air. You never forget the haunting wail of an early morning steam whistle deep in the mist-shrouded hills of southern Victoria.

But there were no mist-shrouded hills on the Long Paddock. It was just a hot narrow strip of bitumen until it got to Mathoura. From there on we were on a gravel road until we got to Deniliquin, and after that it was just dirt tracks for hundreds of miles.

At Deniliquin we left the harness horses safe in the railway trucking yards and rode into Deniliquin. We left our good 'going out' clothes at the dry cleaners, had a feed at a café, whistled at girls for a while, and then rode back to our wagon. Next day we harnessed up and drove the wagon into town to collect the dry cleaning. Of course our stuff wasn't ready, so while I waited in town to pick it up when it was done, Big Neville went on in the wagon. I'd catch up later.

I was walking out of town with our newly cleaned clothes when Snowy Baker's travelling buckjump show headed out of town, so I waved down the lead truck. As I approached, old Ma Baker, as tough as the truck she was driving, stuck her head out of the side window. 'Suppose ya want a lift?' she yelled. I told her that I wanted to catch up with a wagon up the road. 'Climb onto the running board,' she grunted, 'I'm always pickin' up bloody strays'. So up the road we headed, an overloaded truck with a few rouseabouts perched on top of the load and me standing on the running board, with our good going out clothes under one arm and holding on through the open window with the other. At Pretty Pine we caught up to Nev with the wagon and we pushed on towards Hay and the Murrumbidgee River. It was a good feeling to be heading for Banjo Paterson country.

At Hay there was a grasshopper plague; the swarms blacked out the sun to such an extent that the streetlights were on. We stayed for a couple of days with Neville's friend, Frank Dolan, where we enjoyed a few home-cooked meals and comfortable beds. The horses enjoyed the rest, too, and being fed with good grain.

In the pub we got talking to a station owner and Nev, always the dealer, worked out a trade, an 'all purpose' saddle he owned in return for a bay saddle mare. When we hit the road, we called into the station and Nev did the deal. Now we had one more horse with us, but not for long. Nev made a nice profit on it when he sold it to another station owner near Wilcannia.

It was about here that we started to refer to each other as Mick. Maybe I'd be going crook at the horses for no reason with a comment like, 'Get over there, you great big lump,' and Nev would yell to me, 'You tell him Mick!' then it just went on from there. With comments such as, 'What d'ya reckon Mick?' or 'Shut up, Mick, you're snoring', or 'You grab the horses Mick, I'll pack the wagon,' that name stuck all the time we were away. People we'd meet would assume that at least one of us was named Mick, they just didn't know which one.

Before we left Hay we bought our supplies and a bag or two of horse feed, since we didn't know how much the grasshoppers had left. The harness horses were working well and the saddle horses, well they had just come along for the ride, but we wanted to keep them in good condition and the grazing was getting pretty thin. As well, we bought a bag of butcher's salt – this was to wash down the shoulders of the workhorses to avoid scalding from the collars.

Travelling with harness horses day after day it is best to vary their gait. You don't have them just walking for too long, especially in hill country; you trot them along every now and then to get the blood circulating. As you approach a hill, give them a slap with the reins and nudge them into a trot; have them point their ears to show an interest, otherwise half way up the hill they might just grind to a stop and say, 'Bugger this, it's too bloody hard'. But never knock your horses about ... get to know their limits, work out your day's travel, and if it is very hot make sure you don't overwork them. Care for them and be sure they get plenty of feed, water and rest. On the road we'd walk for a while, jog for a while, trot out for a spell and, if we wanted to get somewhere in a hurry, we'd click our riding horses into a canter.

We didn't dwell on, it but 'Clancy of the Overflow' was never far from our minds…snippets like 'Where I'd met him, down the Lachlan, years ago …' but when we stopped on the banks of the Lachlan River next day, other matters took our attention. Nev and I had just lit a fire when one of us looked down and saw a huge red-bellied black snake. 'Wot we gonna do with it?' said one of us. 'Dunno,' said the other, 'maybe we orta try the local fare'. One of us hit it with a shovel, I skinned it, gutted it and cut it into bite-sized pieces and Neville cooked them on the open fire. I guess it went down well with a billy of tea. I don't remember.

Once you leave the town and the common land you are in station country. The land is fenced to separate different properties or to divide the stations into paddocks, and these fences cross the road. At the fences there are ramps, or cattle grids, for motor traffic; for travellers with stock there are gates.

If you are travelling with horses north from the south, you camp on the north side of the fence. For them to get enough to eat they'll graze right into the night, and if there is no fence to stop them they'll walk back to the last camp. So you hobble them north of the fence, bell one or two and just let them graze. You might wake at night and wonder where the horses are … you listen, and hear the faint clatter of a bell as a horse shakes his head. 'Huh, huh,' you think, 'they're OK,' then you go back to sleep.

Sometimes you might be camped on good green feed near water, and the horses would choose at about two in the morning to start grazing right in the camp, likely with a loud CHOMP, CHOMP, CHOMP next to your ear, with the bells clanking at each CHOMP. Whoever woke up first would yell 'SHADDUP,' and chuck a boot at them. You'd hear the thunder of hooves and the CLANG, CLANG, CLATTER of the bells as they scattered in their hobbles. Next morning you'd get up, find your boots, and then go find the horses. It was no bother; you'd just pack up camp and harness the horses and be on your way.

When Banjo Paterson wrote the poem 'Hay, Hell and Booligal' he was talking about the One Tree Plain, and it took us three days to cross it. It is about fifty miles (80 km) of black soil, dead flat and you can see forever. One night we were using the cattle grid on the road to hold our pots as we cooked, when I saw the headlights of an approaching car. I grunted, 'Headlights coming'. 'She'll be right,' came the nonchalant reply from Nev, who was cooking. He was right. We'd eaten dinner, made a cup or two of tea and let the fire burn down when finally, in a cloud of dust, the car rumbled by. That's how flat One Tree Plain is.

The black soil of the plain is typical of a great deal of the country from there to the gulf, and we found out that when it rains nothing moves. When it stops raining and you try to move, the vehicle tyres and the horses' feet build up with layers of the sticky black mud, and you also gain several inches in height. You spend time cleaning out the horses' feet and scraping your boots clean before you climb back into the wagon. Then you'd climb back down again, do some other chore, clean off your boots and climb back in again. But everything worked out all right...wet for a day or so, and we soon dried out again.

We didn't have the luxury of a dog, but when we saw a small mob of hoggets along the way, lanky Neville was a good alternative. As we rode in close to the mob he slid off his horse, threw me the reins and said, 'Watch this!' He entered the mob running like a greyhound and emerged holding our dinner by the hind leg. We dined on fresh 'jumbuck' for the next couple of days. This way we could have lamb chops, something you would never get from a station owner. Neville did the catching and cooking, I did the killing and butchering, and we both did the washing up, whether it was needed or not.

Two young bucks with our horses, what more could we want? And when we reached One Tree Pub we started to feel like we were in the outback. Unlicensed since 1942, it was still in good condition, still with its original paint and its mirrored 'Tooths Beer' and 'TB' signs on the outside walls. Back in 1862 it was built as a staging post for the famous Cobb and Co. coaches, carrying squatters and their families to the great sheep stations that dotted the countryside. It must have been a welcome sight to travellers and trades people way back in the horse and buggy days, and of course to the bullock drays too. And during the great depression, I'll bet many a swagman was warmed by the comforting sight of the lamps on that same veranda.

There it stood, lonely and alone, on an unlikely road junction in the middle of that arid, almost treeless plain. For a moment we stopped on the road in front to have a look and take a photograph. The only sign of life we saw was someone peering quizzically at us through the doorway, I guess it was Frank McQuade, the occupant. And of course there was the mandatory hapless old Border Collie dog wandering aimlessly along the veranda.

But we were going places. We gave the horses a click and were back on the road to more adventure … and adventure we got.

We were travelling through Lignum country and we'd seen quite a few wild pigs scurrying through the saltbush and scrub as we moved along the narrow dirt road. We had pulled off the track to make camp at a government tank when Nev spotted a big black wild boar trotting across the road quite close to us. 'Grab your rifle,' he yelled, 'I'll turn him back to you'. As he slipped easily onto his young grey riding horse and cantered bareback towards the pig, I picked up my 38-40 Winchester, sliding bullets into the magazine as I jogged easily towards them. The one thing we learned by what happened next is that you can't stop a wild pig with a horse.

Nev loped easily past the pig and then tried to turn it around. Big mistake! This massive boar went straight on under the horse, knocking its legs out from under it. On seeing the horse and my pal crashing to the ground, I levered a round into the chamber as I broke into a run through the shoulder-high grass. I hit the clearing only to see the horse on its side, Neville on the ground, and the boar no more than a body length from them making its charge. I was close, and able to get one snap shot away on the run. To our good fortune that one shot got the razor-back right behind the shoulder and killed him outright. Yep! We both learned something that day.

Somewhere on the track to Wilcannia we met Lofty Cannard and his crew. They were walking a mob of NSW station horses down to Melbourne, untried horses that were to be sold as riding hacks to anyone silly enough to buy them. The horses were being held in a set of government yards, and Lofty's crew were camped nearby.

Mick and I spent the night with them, talking and swapping yarns, and we told them of Nev's encounter with the wild pig. Then Lofty's wife Shirley, who had been listening while she cooked a meal for the lot of us, spoke up quietly and said, 'You got off lightly'. She lifted the hem of her dress to show us the great fresh scars on her shins and the still purple marks of fifty stitches in each leg. She had been set upon by a wild boar. Luckily there was a bull terrier in the camp and that dog fought the pig for half an hour. It chewed off both the pig's ears and held it at bay until somebody despatched it with a rifle. No doubt that dog saved Shirley's life. I would not like to think what could have happened to Nev had I missed with that one snap shot back in the Lignum.

Then we met Arthur Clifford and his kids. They were a family of drovers returning from a sheep droving trip, on their way back to their home base on the Wilcannia common. We met up and camped with them a few days, clowned around and put on a whip cracking show. Nev jumped up, swung the whip around, gave it a fancy crack and declared 'I'm Spinifex Mick from Crabhole Crick'. The name 'Spinifex' stuck, and from that time on he had a choice of three names.

Next morning we travelled with them and Arthur's cut-down Concord stagecoach, a striking vehicle that had once belonged to Cobb and Co. There was Arthur at the reins of his four-in-hand team and Nev, alias Spinifex Mick, high up beside him riding shotgun. I reckoned we looked good travelling in convoy ... Arthur and Mick on the big wagon, me driving our little wagon and Arthur's kids bringing up the fifty or so drover's plant horses and a spring cart in the rear.

Approaching Wilcannia we were crossing a big sheep station when we pulled up for a lunch break as. After we'd cooked and eaten we saw Arthur and the kids building up their cooking fire into a huge bonfire, which seemed strange on such a hot day. Then all of a sudden the dogs and the kids went off, cut out a small mob of sheep, and through the dust each kid emerged with a sheep by a hind leg. In no time at all the sheep had been killed, skinned and dressed and the evidence was now on this huge bonfire.

A few minutes later we saw a trail of dust as the station owner headed our way. When she reached us all she could say was, 'Make sure you put out your cooking fire when you leave'. Yeah, we left all right; Nev and me, straight away in our own little wagon, glad to be separated from the sheep herders. No way did we want to get sprung for sheep stealing.

Soon we drove proudly over the bridge into Wilcannia and pulled up outside the great general store, Knox and Downs. At Wilcannia we decided to increase the horsepower of our wagon. We bought a suitable piece of timber for a wagon-pole, cut off the shafts, fitted our new pole to the shaft fittings and fitted the swingle bars (we had managed to scrounge one) to where the shafts had been. A swingle bar is a swinging cross bar on the wagon where the traces are attached; this gives movement and makes it more comfortable for the horses. The wagon was now set up for two-in-hand. Using our spare harness, and with the reins set for double, we put our two best horses on the pole and drove around the town to show off and give it a trial run.

We stopped at the corner pub opposite the post office and got into conversation with Arthur Clifford's dad, Peter Clifford, a big friendly drover who would buy you a drink as soon as you met him. When we said we were looking for work, he told us that they wanted men at Copago, up on the Paroo.

The next day we checked the horses' shoes, harnessed up and drove out of town. We were feeling great as we headed out to Copago to start work.

CHAPTER 5

Kidman country

The Paroo was a romantic name to us, from our schooling and the Henry Lawson poem 'The Paroo River', where he tells of it being so dry they didn't know if they'd reached the river, crossed the river or were standing in the bloody river.

Copago had once been part of Sir Sidney Kidman's favourite station, Momba, and covered about 128,000 acres (52,000 hectares). A fair lump for two kids to look after. We were met in the station yard by Cecil Johnson, one of the sons of the station owners, who lived for most of the time in Wilcannia with his wife and a young family. He was big, friendly and nicknamed Pluto.

We were left for long periods to do all the station jobs that had to be done every day. This was a great life; we were the only employees for a few months and all we had to do was milk the cows, do the killing and butchering, check the windmills, clean the troughs, repair fences, cut fire wood and generally keep the place in good order. We had a couple of old Land Rovers and an International truck we used to get around for the maintenance and we had horses for the stock work. So that was it, no experience necessary.

Over the road was 'Tillenberry', a station owned by Bob Leckie, and the station down the track was 'Purnawilla', belonging to Ross, a brother of Pluto. 'Noonamah' station was further north and belonged to Dick, another brother, who delighted in buzzing us in his Auster whenever he was flying back home from Wilcannia. Dick must have been a hell of a pilot; we were told that he flew his plane under the Darling bridge at Wilcannia – there was no side clearance, so he had to tilt the plane to get it through

As well, we were sometimes sent out to different stations in the district, mostly doing work with sheep. We'd do jobs like marking and docking, crutching, or working in the woolsheds as rouseabouts, where we'd be picking up, skirting and rolling or pressing wool. Or our jobs would be to muster paddocks, fill yards and 'push up' for the shearers.

We were housed in the unlined, concrete-floored ripple iron clad shearers' quarters, but we had meals in the big house; either cooked by Nev or by Pluto whenever he was in residence. Later we were joined by a yardman, another Mick and his wife Mona, who took up the chore of cook and housekeeper. They were good company; we'd play cards at night, or Mona would produce her guitar and we would have a song or two.

Those days very few people used telephones; the services were manual in all but the big cities. To make a call you'd pick up the receiver and wind the handle, the girl in the exchange would ask 'Number please?' and then connect you. The telephone lines to the properties were miles of fence wire strung between trees or bush poles. Not so bad in timber country, but a hazard in open country when strung between low mulga trees and stumpy poles. The wires were strung at about throat height when you were on horseback; which made them especially perilous during mustering. The cattle would be milling around in a great cloud of dust, and if you didn't look up just at the right time you might get your hat knocked off…or even worse.

We found Wilcannia to be a great little town. We had a few friends there and we'd visit whenever we had the chance. We were in the big main pub one time when in stormed the ebullient Bluey Diamond, who was in Wilcannia to buy horses. He had advertised a newly walked down mob of station horses for sale as riding hacks from a rented paddock just out of Melbourne.

Neville and I had worked with Bluey in Melbourne, and

we knew his system. In the Saturday livestock columns the horses would be advertised in some paddock right in the middle of nowhere. First thing Saturday morning the horses would be yarded, and when people turned up to buy Bluey would size up a potential buyer. 'Sir!' he'd say, 'I have just the horse for you, a gentleman's hack'. Then he'd say to one of us, 'Neville or Hoody, catch that chestnut and give this gentleman a demonstration'. We'd catch the horse, throw on our saddle, climb aboard, and if the horse went along anything like decently it was sold. If by chance it went off like a stick of gelignite – and there were good odds – Bluey's words would be something like, 'No boys, not that one, get the one with the blaze'. And if all went right, he had a sale.

I was about to leave one of these sales when I realised that my crupper was on a saddle on one of these unknown horses, but it had thrown its rider and bolted at full gallop for parts unknown. The paddock was a few hundred acres surrounded by light bush on three sides and the Hurstbridge railway line on the other. I leapt onto my own horse and took off in hot pursuit. The horse jumped the fence into the bush, so I jumped after it. We were level pegging as we galloped headlong through the trees and scrub, when suddenly it swung around and headed back for the paddock. We were jumping the fence side by side when

I realised that after a quarter of a mile of open grassland the next fence would be onto the railway track. 'Bugger this,' I said to myself, so as soon as we landed I reached over and grabbed it around the neck, slid off my own horse and hung on. The horse and I crashed in a heap and all I could do was just keep hanging on till a couple of other kids took off the saddle. I let the jug-head go, rescued my crupper, and with a grin I rode off. I had forgotten the event until Bluey blurted it out in the pub at Wilcannia. But I was personally pleased that no one wanted a demonstration.

Every now and then a new lot of workers would descend onto the place to do one of the many tasks that periodically come up on a mixed station. There would be the cattle men with their cantankerous horses, or shearers with their cantankerous cooks, but it added colour to our lives. At shearing time we'd muster the paddocks, or we'd be filling yards and pushing up.

During the big shearers' strike we were never allowed into a union shed because we weren't in the bloody union, but we ate with the shearers, talked to them in the evenings and listened to their anecdotes, stories and complaints. It was my job to keep fresh meat up to the cook, and I was able to kill and dress a sheep reasonably well. Then one young shearer who'd worked in an abattoir taught me how to do the job neatly and in very quick time. I was always learning something.

Then one day Bluey, Lofty and a band of followers descended on the place to buy horses. There were plenty of them, not brumbies but station horses running wild. They didn't all belong to this station, many were owned by drovers and contract musterers from around the district, but because the fences on the property were so run down, the horses were scattered in bands all over the place. Bluey was buying, so the owners all turned up to lend a hand.

Everyone was there at first light next day when we headed

to the stockyards and mounted our horses; Pluto, his brother Ross, Bluey, Lofty and their crew, plus a few of the horse owners, and of course Neville and me. Our purpose was to clear a paddock or two or three and put these horses into a holding paddock until we were ready to drive them to the horse paddock. Then they would be held on good feed and water in a smaller paddock until the time came for Bluey to buy.

It was a busy few days, especially for Nev and me, as the station chores still had to be done – the cows had to be milked, there was cooking to be done, and fresh meat had to be killed. That's how it went for a few days; we would return to the homestead to eat, shower and sleep and continue next morning.

They were a disparate lot, the young kids who had come with Bluey's outfit. One kid they called Boofhead, for very good reasons, wanted to watch me as I killed and dressed a couple of sheep. I did the deed and had just skinned the first beast when I realised the kid was getting a kick out of it, saying things like 'Look at all the guts,' and 'When you gonna take out its gizzards?' He was getting to be a bit much, so I deftly slit the carcase up the middle, reached inside and cut everything free. I called the kid in close and said, 'Here Boof, hold this,' as I placed everything into his cradled arms. For a moment he stood there holding the paunch, half a mile of intestines and everything else until he turned green, dropped the lot, spun around and ran. Boofhead didn't bother me in my chores after that.

We got the horses gathered, yarded and sorted, a price was agreed at twelve pounds ($24) a head, and the horses were put together for the long walk to Melbourne.

Some time later Nev and I walked into the bar of the corner pub at Wilcannia and there was the ebullient Bluey, same blazing red hair, battered old hat and big broad grin. He was back in town talking horses and boasting as usual about what good riders his crew were. Someone yelled, 'I've got a horse in the stockyards I'd like to see youse ride' (really, of course, he was saying he had a horse he'd like to see throw somebody). Bluey was equal to the challenge. 'There y'are, here's a couple now,' he said, 'ride anything, these boys. Ya got your saddles, boys?' 'Yeah, Blue.' The bar emptied as, followed by half the town, we headed to the stockyards. 'That big raw-boned brown gelding,' said someone, 'that's the one, get a halter on 'im'. But in the cloud of dust from the small mob of horses in the yards, no one could get near the horse.

It was then I learnt another lesson. An old black man who had been watching from the fence climbed into the yard saying, 'That's no way to catch a 'orse!' He went on, 'Just pretend he's not there, look through 'im, walk on past and bump into 'im, slide your 'and up under 'is neck … now gimme a 'alter', and with that he had the horse caught. 'Look past 'im, not at 'im.' I never forgot that old boy's words.

We put Nev's saddle on the horse, girthed it up and fitted the crupper. Nev took the lead rope and stepped aboard. There was about a two seconds pause before he gave the lead rope a tug to one side and a slight touch with the spurs, and then all hell broke loose. That bloody horse could buck; it let out a roar and took  a mighty leap of faith straight up into the air. Finally it hit the ground with its head between its front legs and its hind legs perpendicular. It was bucking with a vengeance when the saddle started to slip to one side.

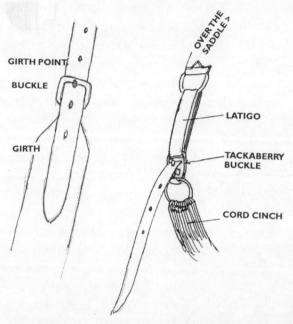

Fortunately for Nev. we had fitted our saddles with a different type of rigging. I had re-placed the original leather girth and strap points with a cord cinch, latigos and a Tackaberry buckle (Bates rig). This way of girthing a saddle onto a horse is super tough and doesn't rely on a strap and buckle. The part called the 'latigo' provides a 'block and tackle' way of tightening the girth, and now was the time to prove its worth. With the horse still going wild, Nev reached under his leg, took hold of the latigo strap and hauled it up another few notches. It was good to watch …and the saddle held. Sort of made me a little bit glad it was Neville that Bluey had nominated to ride.

When the horse finally quit, Nev rode him over and said to the onlookers, 'Now where's that bad horse?'

It was time to muster the cattle for branding, and a crew of cattlemen turned up and moved into the shearers' quarters. This was a chance to get some good experience, so Mick and I just joined in, and we too became cattlemen.

Learning as we went, we mustered each paddock and held the beasts in another holding paddock. There we yarded workable lots, branded and earmarked them, and castrated the bull calves. Many were young and we'd just bulldog them and hold 'em down, but for the rest someone would run in with a noose in a long greenhide rope and drop it over the head of a beast. The other end of this rope would be fixed to a spreader bar, linked to collar hames and traces of the 'bronco horse'. This was a saddled horse with a rider, generally an experienced kid or stockman, who would ride off and slap the beast up against the stockyard fence. One of us would wrestle it to the ground and the other one would handle the hind end. By grabbing the top leg with both hands and catching the other

hind leg with the Cuban heels of your riding boots, you'd lay back and stretch the beast out. Some of these calves, missed in the previous muster, were maybe eighteen months old, about the size of a small rhinoceros, and just as mean, especially when they had just been castrated.

After they had completed their tasks the cattlemen would be on their way, and we would continue doing our own regular jobs, the never-ending routine of maintenance and general care of the stock.

The station was never short of visitors; every now and then family friends of the owners would come and stay to eat and drink for a few days. They'd go out and shoot anything that moved and then they'd go back to their Sydney offices and the place would be quiet again.

One time Cecil's mother, the matriarch of the estate,

came out from her home in Sydney to visit. She had all the appearance of being from fine old colonial stud merino station family stock. During her quite long visit she treated us very well and would invite us to the house for high tea. I remember her telling us, quite seriously, just how lucky we were with our ten pounds a week ... lucky not to have the worry of the woolclip (at that time wool was selling at a record price of a guinea – $2 – a pound) or of selling truckloads of sheep for slaughter or truckloads of fat cattle going to market. We felt comforted by her assurance of how lucky we were not to have money to worry about.

One morning during his mother's visit Pluto came storming out, started the Land Rover, and told the dogs and us to get in. He drove us to the ram paddock and sent the dogs to gather a mob of rams, including some unmarked, un-anythinged old stags, still with a tail and totally feral. We took two of them back to the woolshed, where Pluto said, 'Kill and dress them and hang them in the cool-room'. Those two rams were tough and full of worms, they stunk and were the size of two small ponies.

It seems his mum, the owner, didn't like to see good stud merino two-tooths on the dinner table, so Pluto, in his inimitable way, had set about changing her mind by serving up the toughest old mutton in the state. Next morning Nev said with a grin, 'Take a look at that!' and there was a grim-faced Pluto wheeling out barrow loads of meat to the rubbish dump; he didn't even give it to the dogs. Later that day we got two young two-tooth wethers which I killed, butchered and put in the cool room. All was well after that.

In general, life for us on Copago was one long enjoyable experience ... no ties, no responsibilities, just our horses, swags, rifles and saddles, plus our jobs and wagon to care about. Work was high on the list, for there were animals depending on us, and water is crucial in that dry mulga country. Windmills have to be checked every day or so,

troughs checked daily and scoured out periodically, stock has
to be put onto good feed. We'd use horses whenever it suited,
so we spent a lot of time riding to where the work was to be
done.

That's when you see those sights of the bush that you
never forget, like the huge mobs of kangaroos. Sitting on our
horses, we'd watch those big red males punching the crap
out of each other like prize-fighters, and all those blue-grey
females, hanging around like groupies, waiting I guess on the
result.

There were emus by the score, often standing by their
eggs, and occasionally we'd have scrambled emu eggs for
breakfast. These birds could run like hell; they'd be running
alongside a fence, and we'd be pacing them in a Land Rover.
Suddenly the emu, figuring that if his head would fit between
the wires then all of him should, would hit the fence. He'd
bounce back, occasionally we'd collide and feathers would fly,
but no damage would be done. To save the windshield from
being wrecked we left it folded down, but we'd have to duck
down below the dash or end up with an emu in our lap. Or,
as did happen now and then, an emu would crash in and land
unceremoniously in the back tray.

On those properties there were great areas of paddy
melons growing on the sandy ridges and clay pans; they lie in
the sun until they ferment, and then they're alcoholic. Galahs
in their thousands would descend and gorge themselves on
this fermented melon juice. The time would come for them
to fly home and, using the clay pans as runways, they'd try
to take off. I'm sure I heard them muttering and swearing
to themselves as they blundered forth, flapping their wings
dramatically, only to trip head over heels. Then, mumbling
and swearing, they'd stagger to their feet and try again, and
again ….

One afternoon Mick and I were riding across the station
when we came across a maverick bull in one of the far

paddocks. It was a fair lump of a thing, snotty and scrappy, obviously missed in the last muster. At a time like that station hands like us were supposed to bring an unbranded bull down, earmark and castrate him ready to be branded next muster.

Without hesitation the ever-willing Nev galloped up beside the beast and it immediately took off full chat. Nev's horse and the bull were running shoulder to shoulder when the intrepid Mick deftly reached down, grabbed the beast by the tail and slid off his horse. But the bull kept running and so did big lanky Nev, while his horse took off for parts unknown. As I watched all this unfold I called out, 'Whatcha gunna do now?' 'Dunno Mick,' Big Nev yelled back, 'but grab me bloody horse will ya.' As I took off to retrieve the horse I could see the beast still running flat out and Nev, spindly-legged in his elastic-sided riding boots and strap-legged jeans, determinedly hanging on to the tail with one hand, his hat with the other, and taking giant strides more suited to a big red kangaroo than a tall skinny station hand.

When I returned with his horse I found Neville standing

on one side of a very spindly needlewood tree and the bull on
the other side, circling, snorting and pawing up great clods of
red earth. I poked the two horses between Mick and the bull
and threw him the reins. He took his horse and mounted on
the run, saying 'We'll pick him up next branding, yeah, that's
what we'll do'. Then came the analysis, 'I think I should've
thrown me leg over his tail and flicked him over, or maybe
brought my horse around in front of him and dragged him
down'. We never did work out an easy way, except maybe
pick beasts that are not the size of a Morris Minor car. Then
again, we sure had a lot of fun trying.

We were never short of something to do. If ever we were
out working and we saw a big percentage of sheep in a
paddock showing fly strike, we'd yard them, see that they had
water, and early next morning we'd be back with hand shears,
a container of strike paint and a cut lunch in our saddlebags,
plus our quart pots and a neck bag each of drinking water. All
morning we would work, only stopping to wash our hands,
light a fire, have our lunch and a cup of tea, then it was back
to it again. We'd work until sunset, turn the sheep out to
pasture and ride for the homestead. By this time we knew
every road and track on the place, and as we neared the big
house, we would hear the comforting thump, thump, thump
of the diesel generator sounding like a welcoming friend in
the night.

After putting our horses away we'd go to the house, and
there on the great kitchen stove would be big hot meals sitting
over pots of simmering water. The one thing I remember so
vividly was how the colour of the meal stood out. We had
been in darkness since sundown and there was this beautiful
meal waiting for us. We'd wash, have dinner, relax and maybe
read for a while, have a shower and crawl into our bedrolls.
Who could want more?

About now we let the boss know that we were planning to head north to Queensland. That was OK with Cecil, but as there would be mustering soon for crutching, he'd like us to stay for that. 'Oh, and while you're here you might as well clean out the tank at Salt-Well,' he said.

Salt-Well paddock had a hand-dug well that we were told was two hundred odd feet deep and timbered. The well had a windmill with a thirty-five foot wheel and a five-inch pump to push the water from the bottom into a six-foot deep and fifteen foot diameter holding tank. The storage tank was full of suspended green slime and the water could be contaminated, so it had to be cleaned out. It had no drain plug, so Pluto showed us how to empty the tank by siphoning out the water, and he left us to it. Spinifex and I climbed into the tank with buckets and found that under a thin layer of green algae we were standing in a foot deep of putrid, black, slimy gunk.

At this time we were both down to shorts and gumboots, and just as we got started I heard, urk, urk, urk, from Big Nev. He could handle most things, but the stink here was just too much for him. 'Stay on the outside,' I told him, 'and I'll hand the buckets up to you; that way if you feel like chucking you can just go ahead'. 'OK,' said Nev, 'good idea'. So that's how we did it. Now and then I'd get Nev to turn on the mill just long enough for me to cool off and wash off some of the gunk. Spinifex never did throw up.

We'd emptied the tank, turned on the mill, and I was showering off some of the gunk when Neville said 'Have a look at this!' and there was a pile of small seashells and petrified fish bones that had been brought up in that ancient salty water by the mill pump.

At about this time we got some heavy rain and, thinking of the long trip ahead, we parked the wagon by the blacksmith shop and did some major modifications. We made it longer and wider and did some extra work on the pole. We had the horses, so we scrounged what extra harness we might need from the place. The pole fitting we had was for four-in-hand, so we ran a chain through from where the lead swingle would be to the rear axle, just in case.

While we were there we had a couple of mighty dust storms and one afternoon while I was working on the wagon Mick suddenly said, 'The joint's getting a bit dirty, I'm gonna clean the place up whether it needs it or not'. So he took a big bass broom and started to shove the sand out and sweep the floor. A short time later he let out a yell, 'Look at that!' 'Bloody what?' I said. Mick pointed to the floor and exclaimed 'Bloody concrete!' I guess you just get used to it; with all the dust we hadn't seen the floor for some time.

It was a good thing that Mick had cleaned up the place, for next day who should turn up but the friends we had partied with all those months earlier when we were only a week into our journey north. This time our friends were on foot … somewhere between the mail box and the house they had done the one thing you learn early not to do in the bush. They'd left the track to go around a puddle and they'd gotten themselves well and truly bogged. But it was good to see them, so after the handshakes and g'days we all piled into the better Land Rover and headed off to see what we could do. There it was, sitting just off the track, John Henry`s immaculate Oldsmobile, looking quite forlorn up to its hubcaps in the soft moist red sand. With shovels and a good long chain we freed the beast, drove it to the station yard and parked it in front of the shearers' quarters, where it would stay for an extended period.

Our mates had intended to come for a week and drive back home the way they'd come, down the Cobb Highway through Deniliquin, but the rain kept bucketing down. We just went on with our work and enjoyed their company while they waited for the track to town to dry out. Chirnie was there and gave us all haircuts, and they helped us around the place as much as they could.

A farrier with his hat full of nails.

1962. About to leave for a rodeo, where I'd deliver my latest saddle.

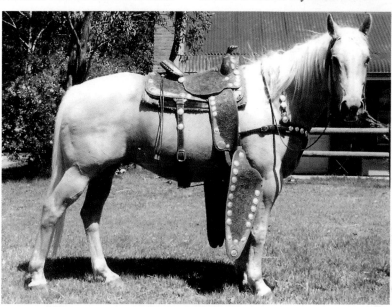

Doc modelling a parade saddle. He knew he looked good.

i

Along the stock route on my first droving job; the boss drover keeps an eye on the mob while they rest and cool off in a dam.

Crossing the old bridge at Echuca.

End of the day. Spinifex unharnessing near Booligal.

Drover Arthur Clifford approaches Wilcannia in his cut-down former Cobb & Co. stagecoach, with Spinifex riding shotgun.

Nev befriended a Joey while we were at Wilcannia.

Buffalo River. Walking the cattle to be flown to Indonesia.

Chet and me,
Buffalo River,
1973.

Keeping the cattle cool at Darwin, en route to Indonesia.

Sundance and me at Tapos, Indonesia. By that time he knew who was hoss and who was boss.

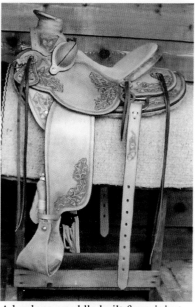

A buckaroo saddle built for reining and natural horsemanship. All the intricate tooling was done freehand.

Photo opportunity at Booligal. We kept out horses fit.

Spinifex about to have his bones rearranged in one of Copago's demonic Land Rovers.

Henry Miller's posh Oldsmobile bogged on the track to Copago.

Trophy of the day. Young Col with a couple of metres of brown snake.

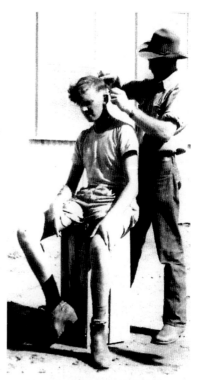

Chirny tidied us up with a short back and sides. It was Big Nev's turn.

We needed 4 h.p. when the going got rough..

President Suharto watches proudly as his
grandson, Ari, tests his new Col Hood saddle.

Indonesia 1973. Taking a
break from teaching
Sundance manners.

Missy in a street parade in Euroa, near Balmattum. She was a
perfect match for Doc.

Not the usual way to be on a horse, but Chiquita, Robyn and Glenn don't mind.

Working on a saddle for President Suharto of Indonesia. Remember sideburns? Photo: Tiff Rainer.

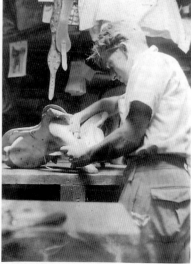

Rawhide covering my first saddle tree.

The saddle ordered by R.M. Williams for cowboy showman Kit
Carson. Photo: Bennie Cologan.

Heading north.

My dad took this photo in 1957, the day I proudly rode Ginger home to show off the first saddle I made.

Caught in the 1956 floods, Paroo River, NSW.

The One Tree Pub, NSW, 1955.

Trying out one of my harness horses, South Morang, Victoria.

While our friends were on the place we took the chance to show them the huge woolsheds built back in the days of Sir Sidney Kidman. Built by men using axes, adzes, crosscut saws and augers, all those great buildings, with anything from fifty to a hundred stands, were constructed using materials from the property. The massive support posts of bull oak, the mighty ridge pole adzed square and hoisted some thirty feet above the woolshed floor, the great rafters of the steeply pitched roof and the pens of morticed mulga rails, were certainly impressive. The boys, especially John Chirnside, my teacher of saddlery, were all awestruck by these wonderful examples of bush carpentry.

Behind the blacksmith shop was the great wool wagon, with all the bullock yokes and chains left where the bullocks were last unyoked at the end of World War II, ten or so years earlier. It seems that all the trucks on the place had been confiscated for the war effort, fuel was near impossible to buy, but the wool had to get to market. With typical bush resourcefulness, a team of work bullocks was broken in, the wool wagon was greased up and the yokes and chains were put in good order, and the station's wool clip had transport. It was hard going in that soft, sandy country to Wilcannia. Pluto showed Mick and me deep wheel ruts, still visible all that time later.

By the time the track to town had dried out the Darling was running high and over the bridge, so our friends had to drive to Melbourne via Broken Hill. They sure had an extended break.

It was time for us to go too. Pluto gave us the report that Bunker Creek was running backwards, so we wasted no time. That same day we drove into town to the big store and stocked up on supplies. We got all the essentials, including a bag of butcher's salt, horse shoes and nails, some kerosene for the lamps, and a bag of feed, just in case.

I finished shoeing the horses as Mick finished loading, we harnessed and hooked a pair to the wagon pole and drove around to the homestead to shake hands with Pluto. As he wished us all the best for the trip he handed us a tin of vulcanizing patches and the clamp thing everybody seemed to carry those days. We were later to be very thankful for this seemingly small gesture.

Then, with a yip and a gentle slap on the rump with the reins, the horses leaned easily into the collars, we heard the familiar creak of the harness and we were on our way. We were as keen as the horses to cover new ground and to see new things.

CHAPTER 6

Up the Paroo

It felt good to be back on the road again. The horses were fit, and everything seemed just right as we sniffed the familiar smell of sweat from the collars as the horses heated up, and heard the clip clop of their brand new shoes hitting the sun-baked wheel tracks. We were headed up the Paroo on the sandy red track that was the road to Wanaaring and … Queensland.

That's where we were heading, Queensland. A magic name to us, it was the gateway to the real outback. We figured if we got through these floodwaters to Hungerford then we'd be OK. We weren't to know that the rains would hang on for so long, that this was just the start of it.

George Stamford from Momba passed us on the track and, recognising us from when we had done some work there in the past, skidded to a stop just ahead. He'd had a few drinks and just wanted to talk, and when we told him what we were doing he told us to call in and pick up some meat when we passed through.

Bunker Creek was flowing all right, but as Pluto said, it was running backwards. The Darling was so high it was pushing water up and into the Bunker. It was about knee high on the horses, and with the country so big, dry and flat we figured it could push all the way to White Cliffs.

George was his normal self when we stopped at Momba. We camped that night and next morning George said, 'You'd better get going, I just heard that the Paroo is rising up river, and you don't want to get caught'. We lost no time in harnessing the horses and hitting the track.

There had been quite a lot of rain in a short time, enough to flood the place and enough to fill the lake on Copago. In the inimitable way of the bush, and because the lake was now full, Pluto's brother Ross had bought a speedboat. With Ross, decisions were made at a million miles an hour.

The rain that caused the Darling to go over the bridge could have fallen way up in Queensland, maybe Cunnamulla or Charleville, we had no way of knowing, and it looked like there was enough rain up north to start the Paroo flowing. We kept on moving, trying to keep one eye on the river to avoid getting ourselves trapped. Further north, above Noonamah, the road follows the river, leaves the watercourse, takes high ground for a while then drops down again to cross the river.

The channel was running deep at a couple of these crossings. The horses charged in willingly, but soon they were almost swimming and the water was up to the floor of the wagon. I said to Mick as I jumped from the passenger seat, 'Keep 'em going, I'll steady the wagon'. When I hit the water I found we were on a good hard base, everything was OK just so long as we didn't float away.

One of the things we were told was, 'Don't camp in the river bed, even if it is dry'. Rain from two hundred miles north could hit with a wall of water two feet high, and would wash you and your camp away. And if it hit at night you'd be in the crap.

Those days we had no radio, no newspapers, and there was no passing traffic. We relied only on the sparsely scattered sheep properties and the mail truck to get weather reports. We figured that if we got flooded in we could leave the wagon on high ground, saddle a couple of horses and take our swags and spare horses with us. We knew that even if there was no work, we would be welcome at the first station we came to.

Although we had a good stock of vegetables and dry goods, every couple of days we would need fresh meat, so I kept a rifle handy at all times. Nev left it to me to provide the meat. I would shoot a pig, a kangaroo, a wild goat or even an emu had we been hungry enough, but it never came to that. Emu eggs, yes, there were plenty of them, and of course, jumbuck … the ever available stolen sheep.

We were a few days up the river and we'd made camp between a mulga tree and the hollowed out bleached white trunk of a huge fallen coolabah tree. We unharnessed, watered and hobbled the horses, did a bit of unpacking and laid our saddles and bridles over the fallen coolabah. I went off to shoot something to eat and came back with a sucker pig. I soon skinned and dressed it and, being in the bush, I just left the skin, the innards, the head and legs on the edge of camp and hung the carcase in the mulga tree to set.

Meanwhile Nev had lit a fire in a forked section of the fallen tree and had cooked dinner. When it was time to hit the sack, the sky looked a bit bleak so we decided to sleep in the wagon. 'Better put our saddles and bridles over the wagon pole,' said Nev. I said, 'Sure, that'll work'.

Big Neville was no dill. Come morning the giant log was gone and all that was left was an outline of white ash and enough hot coals to cook a bit of breakfast. I said, 'Bloody good thing you thought of those saddles'. Spinifex looked over and said 'Gawd yeah, bloody lucky'.

It had been a good idea to sleep in the wagon that night because wild pigs had been through the camp and dragged off and eaten the remains of poor old cousin Porky.

Fresh meat in that hot, arid land doesn't stay fresh for long, so you butcher it as soon as it sets. You put the choice cuts aside to eat straight away, keep a bit aside for stew, and you dry salt the rest. This is best with beef but we also did it with pig meat and lamb. We'd partly fill a sugar bag with butcher's salt and, having cut the meat into chunks, we'd cut deep slits with a hand knife into the heavy sections so that no piece was too thick to absorb the salt and preserve it. We'd rub the salt in, then put all the chunks into the sugar bag and keep it in the salt until we wanted some for a meal. I don't know how long it lasts but, done properly, it is good for at least a couple weeks.

There is no bread at all when you are on the road, and that's why we carried a bag of flour to make damper. Spinifex was a dab hand at cooking and quickly learned to make a fine damper, which he cooked in a pre-heated iron camp oven. The heat was controlled by sitting the oven on a bed of hot coals and adding or removing coals from the lid. A brownie is the same thing, but you add treacle to the mix. I could make stew or braised steak and onions but I left that fancy stuff to Spinifex Mick. I was quite content to do any maintenance, shoeing, or killing and butchering, so we figured it balanced out.

One time we were following the riverbed and when I saw a group of wild pigs, I grabbed my Winchester and leapt from the wagon with fresh meat in mind. I had picked up only three rounds of ammunition and fed these into the magazine as I approached the pigs, thinking that three shots would be all anybody would need. I took a snap shot at a handy sized sucker – and missed. I took another shot as they ran off, and got the same pig in the hind leg. Wanting to keep my last bullet, I swung my rifle and hit the pig on the side of the head with the butt, but the blow swung open the lever action and ejected my last round. Not good. Determined not to return empty-handed, I grabbed the pig by its good hind leg, and of course it started squealing.

I was now in an interesting situation. I had an empty rifle in one hand, a squealing pig in the other hand, Momma and Poppa and the kids in hot pursuit and, bringing up the rear, a number of their distant relatives. Nev thought that was funny, and he looked back grinning as he whipped the horses to a brisk trot. I put on the pace and reached the wagon a few strides ahead of the pigs. Throwing my pig over the tailboard, I jumped in after it and said, 'Let's get the hell outa here'.

The horses quickly left the pig family behind and a couple of miles up the track we made camp. After looking after the horses I killed and dressed the pig and hung it in a tree to set overnight

Sleeping in the fresh open air under the great luminous slash of the Milky Way, I'd often think, 'I wonder what the poor people are doing now?' Sometimes I wondered how the kids who'd planned to come with us, but opted for the Saturday night dance, were doing back in Melbourne. Years later they told me they regretted their decision. I'd lie there, deeply contented, and drift off to sleep to the comforting clang of a Condamine bell as a horse shook his head to let us know that he and his friends were still around.

Up at first light, we were always busy and never bored. One of us might say to the other, 'What's the time, Mick?' and the other might reply, 'Aw, I dunno, about July I think, give or take.'

Somewhere in that sixty-mile stretch from Wanarring to Hungerford we woke up one morning to find that the wagon had a flat tyre. It was time to reach for Pluto's vulcanising patches. Together the two unstoppable Micks, Spinifex and me, lifted and propped the wagon, took off the wheel and mended the tube. We inflated the tyre, replaced the wheel and finally took out the prop to let the wagon down on all fours.

After all that exertion we decided to have breakfast and make a billy of tea, and after that we packed the wagon … not smart. We had forgotten that, as the sun gets higher and the day gets hotter, horses stop grazing and camp in the shade of a tree. And they won't shake their heads for nuthin', so there were no bells ringing to tell us where they were. We made bigger and bigger sweeps in that thick scrubby mulga country looking for any sign that horses might have been there. Finally we found them, standing like statues, still camped under a tree not a great distance from our camp.

You reckon you're going to kick them up the bum when you do find them, but any animosity towards them goes away. You just wander up and say 'G'day hoss', put on their halter, remove their hobbles and lead them back to the wagon. Then you give them a drink, run a brush over them, harness them and hit the road.

CHAPTER 7

Great weather for ducks

There's a dingo fence that separates Queensland from New South Wales. It was built to keep the dingo problem on one side of the fence. I just couldn't work out which side was which. It is six feet (2 m) high, the bottom half being rabbit netting and the top half dog netting, the same wire but with a bigger mesh. The fence was diligently patrolled and any breaks or weak spots were promptly taken care of, so heaven help anybody who left the gate open. We paused in the gateway to take a photograph and drove through, carefully shutting the gate before we headed the short distance to the town of Hungerford.

We weren't really looking for work, not yet anyway; we wanted to get further into Queensland first. But while we were talking to station workers and shearers in the pub we happened to mention sheep, and that was a mistake. It was right in the middle of the 1956 shearers' strike. 'You been workin'? You're not scabs are ya?' one of them snarled. 'No, no!' we assured them, 'we're cattle men! We don't work with sheep, never worked with sheep, we don't like sheep.' These shearers were bloody tough, and we figured it was wiser not to mention that we'd been working at woolsheds pushing up sheep.

It seemed like a good time to move on, so we stocked up on food and other essentials, climbed up into the wagon, crossed the Paroo for the last time and headed for a narrow, dusty stock track that was a short cut to the north. With my namesakes, the low rugged Hood ranges on our right, we drove on through Boorara station and stopped to ask if they had any harness horses for sale.

The big, tough-looking snowy-headed leading hand on the place said he had some horses to sell, including a big bay mare – and if we could ride her, we would own her.

'Hey Mick,' said Spinifex, 'chuck my saddle on for me will ya, looks like we've got us a horse'. She was a good looking harness mare but she had a nasty streak. Spinifex rode her all right. She snorted, spun, bucked and squealed like a stuck pig, but when the time came to hand the mare over the owner wanted to fight. He said the horse wasn't ours, but we figured it was won fair and square. Finally we settled by buying another harness horse, a good strawberry roan, at a premium price if he'd throw in the bay. We took our horses, turned our backs on Boorara and headed towards Thargominda. 'I'm glad it didn't end up in a fight,' said Nev, 'he was such a big bugger he'd have knocked my bloody block off'.

We filled our water tank from the Bulloo River and went on, hoping to turn west at Windorah and try for Bedourie, but we hadn't expected the floods of 1956 to be so big or the low ground to be so wet.

Just finding the road in parts of that country took some doing. A lot of the track just snakes over vast stretches of almost bare ground scattered liberally with hard red stones and pebbles. It was later that we crossed gibber plains, which look the same but the rocks are bigger. One way to find the road was to follow the glint of the broken beer bottles smashed and shattered to eventually become part of the road. By picking up the glint of sun we were able to drive along and follow these 'crystal highways'.

The extra horses from Boorara worked well in harness and gave our old reliable team a well-earned break, but we struck fetlock-deep mud and hock-deep water in a long and particularly wet section of black soil track. The two horses were straining in the collars, it looked like we were barely moving when, with a crack like a rifle shot, a swingle tree broke under the strain. There we were, stranded in a vast sea of floodwater, and there we'd stay if we didn't replace the swingle tree. We rode back to the last station we'd passed through, I forget the name, and told the station manager our situation. 'Take what you want, boys' he said as he led us to a big old harness shed. We thanked him and loaded the horses we were riding with whatever we needed to get us moving again. Piled high with such things as a swingle tree, collars, winkers, hames and traces and whatever we might need, we must have been a rare sight to see as we rode off festooned with horse gear.

With water up to our knees and boots saturated we were able to replace the broken swingle tree and chuck our newly gained stuff in the wagon. We harnessed our good reliable pair, picked up the reins, eased the horses into the collars and got moving again, following the two deep ruts leading off into the distance. We worked for a week or so on another station, mostly maintenance. While we were there we used the blacksmith shop to fit and hot shoe the horses and to rig the wagon for four-in-hand, using the chain we had fitted back on Copago to set a swingle tree for the leaders. Soon we were ready to leave, and at first light we harnessed the team, Big Nev took the reins, eased the horses into their collars and we were on the track again...with our brand new team and plenty of horsepower.

There are some great people out there, not only station owners who generously gave us gear and food when we needed it, but working men like the two packhorse drovers we met. We had a couple of great steaks with them when we camped the night. They had fresh steak because you can't carry much cooking gear when you're travelling with packhorses, so they just grilled their meat over the hot coals on the fire. They travelled with packhorses because, when they'd finished a droving job and the cattle had been delivered, they could mount up and get back quickly to pick up another mob. Travelling with a camp cook and a cook wagon you are restricted to maybe twenty miles (32 km) a day, but by using packhorses running with your plant, and fit saddle horses under you, you can cover up to fifty miles (80 km) a day.

I don't know where they got the fresh meat, but they told us how we could get it on the track. You first select your steer, shoot him and lay him on his side. Then with a sharp knife you cut three parts around a goodly slab of hide to form a very large flap, remove the cuts of meat you want, then lay the skin back into place and turn the beast over. 'When they find him,' I was told, 'they'll think he died from want of air'. That was the Australian way; everybody survived, nobody made a welter of it, and everyone did their best to conform to the words of the eleventh commandment, 'Though shalt make sure not to get caught'. It is illegal.

Sitting around the fire that night the drovers told us a lot about cattle droving and we hung on every word. Both of us wanted to learn as much as we could, about cattle and cattle country. One thing I remember was their account of what happens when a mob makes a mad rush (in America they call it a stampede). A mob of a thousand head could take fright and, as one, they'd hit full gallop in two seconds flat. They would take all before them, the camp, the wagon, logs, trees, horses, anything in their path. Then, after the rush was finally stopped, would come the task of finding the horses, finding the cattle and putting the mob together again. A head count had to be made before the mob could get moving again. I never did experience one of these mad rushes in the outback, but years later I found out what it was like in southern NSW

We were crossing Mount Margaret station and had been ploughing through fetlock deep mud for three days. The horses were fairly worn out and needed a break. The next morning it was still raining, so we decided to leave the wagon and head for Eromanga, 12 miles further on, in the hope that we could get a room. We saddled two horses, tied on our swags and, leading the other horses, we headed off through the mud. Twelve miles (17 km) in that heavy going probably took three or four hours, I dunno, but we finally made it.

In the bar stood a smattering of tall, lean stockmen with their Cuban heeled elastic-sided boots, spring-side leggings, stockwhips and big hats with their ubiquitous Kimberly bashes. Popular in that northern country, this is where they punch out the crown and drive the edge of their hand to form a long groove down the front. They were leaning easily on the bar, talking in their slow, easy drawl about people they had worked for and places they had been, while they waited for the rain to stop. They were drinking Bundaberg rum, served from a wooden keg on the end of the bar, and if you wanted a beer chaser Phil the barman would sell you a big bottle of Fosters export for ten shillings and four pence ($1), a lot those days. It was almost a pub with no beer.

Spinifex and I got on well with the stockmen, who were an easygoing lot, but the friendly atmosphere was disrupted when a gang of sour looking shearers stormed in and we were reminded that the shearers' strike was still on. They were on strike for ten pounds ($20) a hundred instead of the seven pounds ten ($15) they were currently getting. They had heard that there was a non-union crew working at Kyabra station and they were on the warpath. We didn't say much to them, we had heard that 'scab' talk further back at Hungerford, so we just said we were cattle men. They soon stormed off; they were going to fight someone. Mick and I were glad to see them go.

Early next morning we rode back to Mount Margaret and the wagon, harnessed the team and drove to the pub to say g'day and get water. I was at the rear topping up the tank, Mick was standing at the side talking, when the horses took fright and bolted. I saw Mick go for their heads and get swept aside, but I was able to grab hold of the tailboard, clamber over all the gear and grab the reins. I was sorting out the lines when I looked up and saw that the horses were heading, full gallop, towards what looked like a tree-lined creek bed. I hauled the galloping team into a wide circle and brought them to a trot back the pub to finish filling the tank. Before we left we stocked up at Harry Johns' general store.

The rain was relentless. On really wet sections of the track we'd come to fences and gates where the ground would be too boggy for most vehicles. There would be a few down to the diff, the rest would be left there with the keys in the ignition. In the old Australian way, when the country dried out someone passing through would move the vehicles to higher ground; that was the idea anyhow.

Mick and I came to a boundary fence and there was a station hand in his Dodge ute. He couldn't get past the bogged cars in front, so he'd parked it beside the mail truck on higher ground. He declined our offer to haul him through with the horses, but he found a bicycle on the mail truck and told us that he'd left the keys in the ignition and was riding the bicycle to town. 'Someone will drive my ute in,' he said over his shoulder as he rode off along the track.

'What a great country,' I said to myself.

You realise how far from civilisation you are when you have a close encounter or two.

We'd had our meal and last cup of tea by the campfire and it was time to climb into our swags, which we'd left on the ground by the fire. My swag was pretty simple, just a few grey army blankets in a canvas wrap I had designed, and I had just settled in when I heard a scraping, hissing sound. I said to Mick. 'Did you leave a billy on the fire?' 'No,' he said, 'that's you making that noise'. 'It ain't me, it's a bloody snake,' I yelled. I shot out of that swag like a human cannon ball, followed closely by a huge mulga snake, the biggest king brown I'd ever seen. The noise we'd heard was the sound of the snake's scales scraping between the blankets and the canvas swag cover. Luckily he'd slithered into the outer bit and not the warm centre, where I had just arrived. That was one close call.

Another time, miles from anywhere, we were harnessing up ready to get on the track, and I was putting that spooky big bay mare on the pole. She was the one Nev had ridden and won out of Hungerford. Without thinking, I was standing in front of her when I fed the pole strap through the pole ring and, being used to well mannered horses, I just hauled on the strap to take the weight of the pole. Not the wisest thing to do with that mare. She gave an indignant squeal and charged forward, ripping the harness from the wagon pole. In her flight she knocked me down and, with me under her, she galloped for about twenty feet (7 m) before she spat me out the back. The mare's hind feet had ripped a couple of good gashes across my stomach, but luckily we were lean and tough. I looked down and found no insides were sticking out, so I painted it with the bright blue Eurythmic hobble chafe we had bought in Melbourne, and we mounted a couple of horses and went looking for that bloody mare. We found her next day and took off the winkers and collar.

That was the second time she'd done something nasty. The first time, after I'd nailed on a new set of shoes, she reared back and brought both newly shod front feet down on top of my head. That would have knocked my brains out...if I had any ... but luckily I had put on my hat. With these events in mind, and having other harness horses to take her place, I gave the mare to a passing drover. 'She's a good looking horse,' he said, 'don't you want to keep her?' 'No,' I replied, 'take the old bag! If I need some more horsepower, I'll buy another one'.

Close calls remind you that the nearest town might be a

couple of hundred miles away, and there ain't a doctor down the end of the street. And even when you can call the Flying Doctor your problems aren't necessarily over – Jim, the camp cook on my first droving job, had broken his leg at some earlier stage and they were able to call the Flying Doctor from a nearby cattle station. Coming in to land, the Flying Doctor hit a fence and crashed his plane. I guess the pilot was OK, and I know old Jim survived, but it was tough out there at times.

We were in the middle of nowhere, as so often we were, when we saw a rather unusual truck. It had a large well built back on it, with a set of steps and a door. Emblazoned on the side was 'Honest John – The Man Who Brought Nylon to the Outback'. Yes, way off the beaten track was a mobile clothing store. With a flourish he asked us in and 'The Fastest Tape Measure in the West' promptly took pairs of R.M. Williams jeans from the well-stacked shelf and deftly flicked them onto the counter for us to see. It was all very impressive, and we bought 'R.M.' strap leg jeans, some underpants and a couple of shirts. 'All the best boys,' shouted Honest John as we mounted our wagon and went on our way again.

Heading north we followed Kyabra Creek, which had plenty of water. It is fed from the huge Kyabra watershed and eventually drains into the Cooper. We stopped for a midday break in the shade of some trees not far from a big tree-lined waterhole, unharnessed the horses, walked them down for a drink and hobbled them out on open land to graze. It was a scene of total tranquility until I remembered what I'd seen peacefully sitting on that big billabong. 'What about roast duck tonight?' I said to Spinifex as he dozed on his swag. He grunted.

I was sick of sheep meat. 'Yeah, duck would go down well,' I thought, as I loaded my rifle. Big mistake. My prized thirty-eight Winchester was not a good choice of firearm for shooting ducks. Keeping a low profile, I sneaked close to the water's edge, levered in a shell and, taking good aim on a nice-looking duck, I fired.

The crypt-like silence was shattered as a great sheet of flame and a cloud of smoke shot from the barrel. I guess I still had some old black powder ammunition and had unknowingly used it to load the rifle. The deafening roar from the rifle was almost outdone by the combined 'whoosh' of every single waterbird taking off in unison.

Every pelican and spoonbill, all the ibises, the cranes, the ducks and cormorants left in such a rush that you could almost see the water level drop. At the same time galahs, parrots and cockatoos of all types, with their familiar screeching, took frantically  to the air. The crows and kites joined them, and this sent the brolgas, the kangaroos, the emus and the water chooks in all directions. And, alarmed by this hullabaloo the horses, although hobbled, took off at full gallop for parts unknown.

'What the hell happened?' yelled a bewildered Spinifex as he sprang to his feet. My sheepish reply was, 'Sorry about that! I'll 'splain later. The horses have sorta gone walkabout, we'd better find 'em.' During the two hours it took us to find the horses I explained how it came about. Big, easygoing Neville wasn't bothered and, just like normal, we caught the horses, walked them back to the wagon, harnessed up, and headed north.

The final twist came at dinnertime, when we had to settle for tinned meat. With all the fuss at the billabong, I'd neglected to pick up the bloody duck.

It's easy to lose track of time when you are on the road like we were; one day drifts into the next. Pushing on through the Gidgee, we called in at Kyabra station, mainly to find out the date, because I wanted to go down to Melbourne to be best man at the wedding of my darlin' kid sister, and I knew it was soon. The station hands told us the date and I found I didn't have a lot of weeks to go.

We headed for Springfield station, hoping to leave the wagon and horses there and catch a lift down to Quilpie. At Springfield, the head stockman said, 'Park your wagon over there, put your horses in the horse paddock, that gate over there. Put your swags in the men's quarters, you can camp there and eat in the mess. There's a cattle buyer due here tomorrow and he'll be taking some salt beef and supplies to a drover with a mob of cattle on the stock route to Quilpie. He'll give you a lift.'

It had been quite a while since I had been in a proper bathroom. We had washed in buckets, stock troughs, bore drains, creeks, billabongs and floodwaters, using plenty of soap but not a lot of razor. Being young, I didn't need to shave all that often, and Spinifex even less frequently.

'They've got some wild looking buggers working here' I thought, as I saw a bloke walking past what I thought was a window. I only realized it was a mirror when I walked back and the same rough-looking station hand was walking the other way. I made sure I cleaned up properly for dinner that night.

The roads, more like goat-tracks, were perilously waterlogged so we were glad to see the cattle buyer turn up fairly early. He got his business done with, and we threw our swags and saddles, together with a great sack of salt beef and a sack of flour, into the back of the International ute.

The track to Quilpie passed through Thylungra, a huge sheep property, and six miles from Thylungra we came to a flooded creek. There was no way to cross, and no trees close handy to winch it across, so we were stuck there. The cattle buyer opted to walk to the homestead to get a few good meals and a bed; we camped in a nearby set of stockyards, and knew that our next meal would be salt beef, onions, spuds and damper made in the coals of the fire. There was a rifle in a rack behind the seat of the Inter, and I always carried mine, so I was able to shoot a rabbit or two. Also, we had something different to eat when I found some mushrooms and cooked them in a shovel. We lived all right.

We were there for a week waiting for the water to drop, and in that time I scrounged around and found some long lengths of plain fencing wire that I figured would make a cable. I ran about four lengths between two posts along the stockyard fence and twisted them into a 200 foot (60 m) long rope, which Mick and I then ran from the nearest tree about 200 feet ahead of the vehicle. The creek had dropped to about two feet deep, and we figured the winch could handle the steep, washed-away banks. We were setting up the winch when the driver turned up and in no time, using the heavy-duty winch with its three-foot lever, we were over the creek and on our way.

We called in to Thylungra to let them know we were out of trouble and, once on the stock route, the truck really covered ground. We soon caught up with the cattle and stopped to give the crew what was left of their sack of salt beef. Mick and I stayed in the vehicle while the cattle buyer and the boss drover on his stock horse talked cattle and delivery dates.

All the talking done, the buyer helped sling this great sack of meat over the horse's shoulders in front of the saddle, and returned to the vehicle. The drover was just settling his new load when our driver pressed the starter. It made the noise that starters do, and with that the horse took fright and dropped its head. The last thing we saw as we drove off was this great useless slab-sided hay-burner with its head between its front legs, roaring and bucking over the plain. Still on it was the drover, grabbing for reins, mane, flour bag and gunnysack as chunks of salt beef sprayed out in all directions.

When we got to Quilpie we found that the Bulloo River was in full flood and the last train out, a cattle train, was to be loaded next day. Onto the end of this was hooked an old Victorian era passenger carriage, complete with a small sink, water bottles and an observation platform

First thing next morning Nev and I looked at the rail bridge and there were just two silver strips of the rails showing above the floodwater. We were in the old carriage when the engine let off steam, gave a blast of her whistle and a stamp of her feet and headed for Brisbane. She carefully tip-toed over the river on her narrow ribbon of track, then opened up to maybe a breakneck thirty-five miles an hour.

It was a long trip to Melbourne, involving a fair bit of train-changing … Roma, Brisbane and at the NSW and Victorian borders … 'soon it will be standard gauge all the way through' they said. Well, it happened, but not soon.

Back in the family home there was a lot of talk, and I slept well and long that night. Next day I met up with Spinifex, and while we were talking I nonchalantly asked him. 'How'd things go at home?' Nev snorted back, 'How'd things go at home? I'll tell you how things went at home. You leave the house for five minutes and they rent out your room. I'm sleeping on the bloody couch'.

During the next week or so I spent some time with my folks, related to them some of our adventures, and bought a trendy new suit to wear to Val's wedding, the event that had brought me back. The wedding went well; my darling sister Valerie looked stunning and Brian, my new brother-in-law, looked stunned.

Now I could spend some time with my leather-working, saddle-making friend John Chirnside and continue work on the new saddle I was making. I was keen to get it finished and get back north again. I wasn't yet adventured out.

Nev, AKA Spinifex, must have been even more anxious to get on the road, because when I ran into him a bit later he said to me, 'I'm sick of sleeping on the couch. Lofty has started a travelling tent rodeo, and I'm joining his crew'.

'OK,' I replied, 'I'm sure to run into you somewhere. Best of luck'.

I was packed and ready to jump a train and head north when my dear mother handed me a registered letter saying, 'This came for you today, so I signed for it'. It was my call up to do the next half of my national service. Had it not been signed for, I would have been on a train and heading straight north. Instead, for the next three months I lived in tents, blew things up with explosives, shot at things with machine guns, did the long forced marches and obstacle courses, and of course plenty of the inevitable square bashing.

When I'd finished my stint at 'Scrub Hill' I took a job for a few weeks to make some money to get me back to Queensland. I must have been talking about my plans, because a young fellow named Bill, who had knocked about with us for a while, said, 'I'd like to go bush'.

I guess I must have said to him, 'OK, let's go,' because soon we were on our way to cattle country, the land of Henry Lawson and Banjo Patterson, and droving down the Cooper.

That takes me back to where I started this story … but don't go just yet. I've got a few more yarns about horses and saddles, people and places. So take the reins, and we'll ride together a little longer.

CHAPTER 8

City cowboy

I needed to be able to get around after I returned to Melbourne, so I bought myself a motor bike, and one of the first places I went on it was to Thornbury to see John Chirnside and get back to work on my new saddle. I had come back from my adventures a bit more mature than when I left, but I little knew then what a great influence John Chirnside was to have on the direction my life would take.

I wasn't thinking of a horse, but a while later I ran into Bennie Weir, an old horse trader I'd known for years, and the conversation got around to a horse he'd just bought. 'Just the horse for you,' he said. They've all got 'just the horse for you', but I trusted Bennie. 'Four-year-old chestnut gelding,' he went on, 'sound as a bell and handled, just not broke in'.

I had owned horses for so long that I couldn't imagine myself without having a saddle horse under me. When I looked the horse over I liked what I saw, paid Bennie, got the horse home and started to break him in to saddle. He was well mannered, and in no time I had him saddled and bitted. A few bucks and grunts, and he was ready – ready enough for me anyway.

Now it was time for a set of shoes. I tied him securely to the fence, dropped a handful of shoeing nails into my faithful old Akubra and proceeded to dress his feet. Just as I'd been doing for the last few years, I nailed on all four shoes, clinched them up tight and rasped the feet to make them look neat. Now I had myself a well shod, newly broke saddle horse. Because he was chestnut I named him Ginger, and I owned him for maybe fifteen years; he was always a pleasure to shoe and a pleasure to ride.

Being back in the city was quite a change, but in those days it was safe and easygoing. We could do simple things like ride our horses into the heart of the city to do a bit of shopping. I had most everything I needed; I had my new saddle horse and my motorcycle, I was working at my trade, money was plentiful and so were jobs … if you told the boss to shove it at one place, you could go next door and start a new job without missing half a day's pay. Just like my dad had said, 'You'll always have something to fall back on'.

Many of the friends I had ridden with four years earlier were still about, so there was plenty going on. I wasn't at all interested in the future. All I wanted was to give my chestnut horse a name, get him going well, cover some country in my new saddle and, of course, to have plenty of fun. Rock and roll was here, there were girls everywhere and espresso bars had become meeting places. Chinese cafés were new and they were cheap.

Our old stomping grounds were surrounded by open grassy paddocks, now known as the suburb of Bundoora. A crowd of us would gather at Carlson's, a pretty ordinary livery stable where people would come and rent out horses by the

hour. The place called itself a 'riding school' but people who hired didn't learn much; anyhow, the horses were lazy and quiet so the riders enjoyed themselves without coming to any harm. But for us, the cool ones, it was a handy place to get together, and it gave us somewhere to get out of the rain on a wet winter's day.

I learned very early that a lot of girls were horse mad. There were the girls who owned their own horses, the girls who came out to hire horses and, of course, the girls who just wanted to be around horses … and the guys who owned them. That's why I made sure my horse would take double. If I were to have a girl on the back she might get scared if my horse threw in a couple of piggy little bucks.

We all knew Jack the stable owner; he had been a top jumps jockey in his day. There were a couple of good old vets and horse dentists who used to sit in the office and talk for hours. They'd all been in the Light Horse in the First World War, and we'd listen to their stories of the charge at Beersheeba.

These were the mighty, unforgettable men, the farriers, the vets, the horse dentists and the breakers, who taught us and guided us at that stage of our lives. They all had plenty to talk about, and we'd hang on every word. A good horse breaker taught me how to mount my first unbroken colt (I'd take it a bit slower these days); I learned how to care for the horse's feet. At Carlson's, as the horse dentists were doing their job, we'd have to put our arms right into our horse's mouth and feel the teeth before and after they were rasped.

The chestnut horse I bought from Bennie Weir was going well under my Australian stock saddle, but I couldn't wait to try out the one I was working on under John's guidance

This was a perfect time to start riding western, and the right time to start making western saddles. Western movies were popular, the rodeo boys were showing an interest in going western, and I was doing quite a bit of leatherwork for my own friends, making such things as martingales, bridles, reins, gun holsters, and waist belts. Those jobs were a bloody good sideline that added to my income. Without knowing it, I was travelling towards the life that would be my future.

Every Thursday night a group of friends would turn up at John Chirnside's workshop. We'd sit around, talk horses and cowboy stuff, or we'd tell jokes and sing hillbilly songs. John was a very accomplished guitarist and singer; he'd lead off and we'd sing along or do solos like 'Click Go the Shears', or 'Heartbreak Hotel'. There sure was some noise made in that crowded shed. John was showing me the relevant guitar chords for the songs we sang, but a couple of years passed before I took the time to learn guitar. I had one thing in mind, and that was to play along with him.

Those weekly gatherings were quite separate from the creative time I spent at the workshop, working on my western saddle and making the gear that went with it. A couple of years had passed since I made those two trees, and I was anxious to get the saddle finished, go for a ride and prove a point to myself. One thing was certain – the new saddle would differ entirely from the Australian stock saddle I had been riding in since I first discovered horses.

One Saturday morning I rode my horse bareback down to Thornbury and up the back lane to the rear of John's workshop. It took a few minutes to saddle the horse. Chirnie provided a good Navajo saddle blanket, I put the saddle in place and, for the first time, I 'cinched it down' – that's western for 'I did up the girth'. I stepped on board, adjusted my seating position and settled in.

'Now get going and show it off,' said Chirnie with a smile.

With a huge grin on my face I rode back to our home in Preston just to show my parents. My father had watched this saddle as it was slowly taking shape and was pleased to see it finally completed. Outside the house he took a photograph and watched as I rode proudly off for Bundoora, where I'd meet up with the rest of the crowd.

Everyone I met wanted me to show my saddle to somebody else. It was like nothing they had ever seen before, and it made me proud just to be seen riding down the road. The saddle was basket-stamped all over, giving it the appearance of woven leather. To enhance the horse, I had made a matching bridle and breastplate.

Life was good. When I started using my western saddle so many people wanted one that John and I started making them to order. Orders came from rodeo contestants, pleasure riders and showmen. That started the whole western scene rolling, and it's been growing ever since – now I can say with a grin, 'You can blame me for that'. And for me it was the start of a lifetime's dedication to the western way.

Pretty soon it seemed the word had got around that I was the one to ask if anybody wanted to know anything about western saddles. And anything western I wanted to know, I only had to ask my dear and valued friend John Chirnside, who would give me an accurate and honest answer.

We'd ride our motorcycles to rodeos around the state. I wasn't interested in competing; I wasn't crazy-wild enough. 'To win at rodeo,' John said, 'you've gotta have that killer instinct'. I didn't mind a horse dropping his head and throwing in a few bucks, in fact I enjoyed it, but I just didn't care for the killer bit. I found myself talking more about roping saddles and taking orders. Those days they were all for hard and fast calf roping, which was slowly gaining in popularity.

I didn't have any wish to make money winning rodeo contests; the best way to make money out of rodeo was to build saddles and gear for the contestants. It was a good adjunct to my day job as a patternmaker; after work I was a saddlemaker with John. My daytime patternmaking job was very fortuitous; I could rough out the wooden saddletrees at work, bring the components home and assemble them. Not only that, but I'd make patterns for the horns and the rigging dees and cast them in bronze at the same place.

My friend John Chirnside was New Zealand born, but his family moved to Australia when he was twelve years of age. Like the rest of us, he bought a horse when he was young, 'mucked about' like we all did, and became a fine horseman. He had learned a trade in the delicate and complex electronics field, but had left his profession to take up the pursuit of fine leatherwork.

One of the great old Melbourne saddlers had taught John on the proviso that he'd pass his knowledge on to someone else…and guess what? Over all those years I was the only one who would listen and learn. And learn I did. Not long later we had a fine trade running. I was young and willing, full of get up and go, and John was known as the straightest man in the state.

One of the orders we got from rodeos was a special, vastly different saddle for Stewart Lear. Stewart was a top rodeo rider, Golden Gloves competitor and, at that time, a taxi driver. Now he decided that he wanted to be a trick rider, performing different tricks on the back of a horse at full gallop.

The Cossack drag is one of the acts of the Russian Cossacks. You throw your left leg over the saddle and anchor your ankle high up on the off (right) side of the saddle, then throw your body down on the near (left) side of the horse and have your knuckles almost touching the ground.

We've all seen the Hippodrome stand (hippodrome meaning horse venue) in movies, with the rider standing in front of the saddle and leaning forward to compensate for the thrust…and to look good. You need a specially designed saddle for this, with leather loops high on each side of the fork, or front section.

The shoulder stand is another quite effective but simple act where you take hold of the specially designed saddle horn with your right hand and your left thumb takes hold of the near side corner hold. Once settled, you throw yourself into a shoulder stand on the horse's neck in front of the saddle.

The crupper drag is one of the more perilous acts. Both ankles are securely anchored to the saddle and you lay full length behind the horse, again with your knuckles near dragging on the ground.

To perform these spectacular tricks the first thing needed is a completely reliable horse; the next thing is a specially designed saddle, and John and I got the job of designing and making a safe and exceptionally strong trick riding saddle for Stewart. It gave us a real challenge, something to aim for. I designed and made the tree, including the six-inch high polished brass vaulting horn, John covered the tree with rawhide, and we both built this special-purpose saddle with its rawhide-strengthened corner handholds and holds for the crupper vaults

We also made a superb, fully tooled riding saddle for Stewart's wife, Margaret. At each performance she'd ride to one end of the arena and sit there on her pretty paint horse while Stewart aimed his horse towards her. At full gallop he'd perform each trick, and as his grey horse approached Margaret's paint he'd slow to a canter and stop beside her. The horse behaved a bit like a kid running home to mum. To make it safe and reliable for Stewart, Chirnie and I fitted all the straps and hitches and saw that they had been fully tested. Stewart's tricks had not yet reached the ultimate, there was still one more. There were more straps to make, as well as another saddle.

I was working in a foundry as a patternmaker, but doing both jobs was getting a bit much. There is an old saying, 'Don't give up your day job' but, with all the saddle work I was getting, it looked like I might have to try it out full time.

'You've always got your trade to fall back on,' my dad had said.

John my teacher, although much older and wiser than me, had never married but he had a pen pal in the United States. She lived in Los Angeles, her hobby was leather carving and her name was Marge. She and John must have hit it off because she came out for a visit. John borrowed his dad's car and showed her the state. Of all the people Marge met in Australia, and although I'd never left the country, she said I was the most American person she'd met here. I dunno if that's good or bad.

Marge went back and it wasn't long before Chirney, my dear friend, bought a ticket on an ocean liner and sailed off to be with his love. They were married soon after he arrived. John soon opened a custom made saddle business in San Gabriel, California, and quickly gained the reputation of being one of the finest tradesmen on the west coast.

Now Chirney was gone I had some planning to do. With the basic skills I'd gleaned from my master teacher, I thought 'I'll give it a go for a while and see how it works out'. I seemed to be doing all right; it helped when I started making western saddles and leather tooled articles for the renowned R.M. Williams of South Australia.

It was about then that I had the opportunity to work closer to the city. I was offered a 'garret' in Drummond Street, Carlton, and it was in this loft above a stable that I started to make the trophy saddles for the famous Mount Isa rodeo.

There are a few countries where rodeos are part of the popular entertainment scene – the USA, Canada, New Zealand and Australia. The rodeo boys themselves are lean, tough, wiry, basically honest and good to animals. I believe that whenever a new crop of rodeo boys are requested, an order is put in for, say, fifty. When they are about to get born, God (or whoever dishes them out) will say: twenty to America, twelve to Canada, ten to Australia and eight to

New Zealand. Most of the bigger rodeos present a trophy saddle to the winner of the main event, Open Saddle Bronc. Mt Isa Mines would donate the saddle and the Rotary club would present it to the winner.

The Mount Isa orders started off with one trophy saddle for each rodeo. In the finish I was making trophy saddles for three separate events, and I made these trophies for twenty years and more. I also had the income from my regular local work, anything from saddle repairs to making reins, bridles, gun holsters and waist belts, which kept me going between saddle orders. These were either from rodeo boys who were gaining interest in western saddles, or orders from R.M. for his mail order business.

One memorable order from Reg Williams was to build a saddle with matching bridle, breastplate and matching double six-gun holsters for Warner Bros. cowboy actor, Kit Carson. Kit wasn't a household name, but he sure was a very impressive man, standing seven foot two inches (218 cm) from the ground to the top of his ten-gallon cowboy hat. All the gear I made for him was fully floral tooled and trimmed with silver-like adornments, called conchas – it certainly was quite an outfit. I got to know Kit when we'd run into each other at different shows and rodeos. He sure dressed to stand out, just like another old customer, Chief Little Wolf. I got to know the Chief when John and I did some work for him. He'd fill the workshop, and whenever I'd see him in his 1955 Ford Mainline ute with the Indian head-dress painted on the driver's door I'd give him a wave and yell, 'G'day, Chief.'

I was working in the loft when Stewart Lear introduced me to the great newspaper photographer Bennie Cogolan, who came in to photograph the saddle I'd made for Kit Carson. I got to know Bennie, and sometimes I'd go down to the Herald and Weekly Times building where he'd perform his magic. In those days photography was a completely hands on, skill-oriented profession and to watch Bennie work was

like watching an alchemist. Other times Bennie and I would
repair to the corner pub and lean on the bar to talk and drink
with the reporters.

People were always calling in to the loft; there seemed
no end to it. A regular visitor was Joe Allison, a well-known
name in Melbourne, and he had a story to tell. Back in 1942,
when invasion by the Japanese seemed imminent, huge
mobs of cattle were walked across the top end from the big
Kimberley stations to the relative security of Queensland.
The drovers became known as the Overlanders; Joe was one
of them and he loved to tell the stories

Joe had a tack room full of very high quality American
saddles and I would visit to talk and to study those saddles.
Just seeing and touching them gave my own work a boost. He
had some saddles made by Hamley of Pendleton, Oregon – I
used an illustration from a Hamley catalogue when I made
the tree for Stewart Lear's trick riding saddle.

Some say a good saddle has to be broken in – they say,
'ride in it all day ... every day ... forever'. Top horseman Max
McTaggart used to say 'Chuck it in the horse trough, then
ride in it all day, that'll break it in'. I inadvertently found a
third way when I was down on Wilson's Promontory on a long
ride. I came to a wide creek and, assuming it was shallow, as
it had been downstream, I rode my horse Ginger smartly up
to the water's edge and he boldly stepped in. We both went
straight to the bottom, and both came up snorting water and
wondering what had happened. It was a learning experience

for both us. The creeks way down there run a coffee colour because of the Mesquite scrub run-off, and what I should have remembered that day was that shallows, running over the white sand, are almost clear, and the water is darker as it gets deeper. Where we went in was a very dark burnt umber.

We swam to the other side, and as it was a hot day I stayed in the saddle and finished the day's riding. That saddle was certainly well broken in. Because the saddle is cinched or girthed firmly down on a good saddle blanket, the dense high quality woolskin lining holds out all water except for maybe a little around the edges. It sure worked for me that day.

That year, 1958, was a year of changes for me. I had started to work for myself. I'd made some great gear and met some very interesting people. Girls, instead of being a fleeting aside, were beginning to become more meaningful.

It was a big change, too, not to have John Chirnside around for friendship and advice. In one of his letters he told me that some guy stormed into the shop and asked, 'Where are all these custom made saddles I've been hearing about?' John's reply was, 'The customers have got them'. Well, of course. Just as a bespoke tailor doesn't have racks full of custom made suits, when a custom made saddle is finished, the customer comes and picks it up; it doesn't sit on the rack.

John was a fine saddlemaker, and before he left Australia he said to me, 'Wait a couple of years until I settle in, and then come over and work for me'.

One of my greatest regrets in life is that this never happened.

CHAPTER 9

A new lifestyle

There were plenty of girls around, especially for guys with a horse and a motorbike. I was attracted to a pretty young blonde who kept her tall bay thoroughbred at Mack's place. I asked her out to a dance and from then on we saw a lot of each other. We'd ride together, and if we wanted to go on a trip we'd go by motorcycle. The laws were a little less rigid those days, and with those English bikes a hundred miles (160 km) an hour was a big thing. Our 'mad mile' was between Janefield and south Morang and I was quite proud to have done a 'ton' on that stretch, especially with the same girl riding pillion. But to go out on Saturday nights to dances or the pictures, I'd pick her up in a taxi and bring her home the same way.

Her name was Frances, we liked each other's company, and we even joined up with some of the old crowd who had started a saddle club just out of Gisborne, Victoria. My outlook was on the change. I bought a 1950 two-door Silver Streak Pontiac and we got around in style.

I hadn't been spending a lot of time in the loft, just staying with my parents and using the loft for work. Then I got a phone call, 'Come down to Drummond Street and salvage what you can'. Some kids had set fire to the stable below, and the loft had burned. Any leather and saddle work was destroyed, but the loss could have been worse. My tools were scorched but OK, my cutting and carving tools were all good, and my sewing machines were ready to be used next day.

From home I set up just enough to get me through, and took a job in my trade. It was good to get a wage packet instead of relying on the whims of customers. I put my saddlework on the shelf for a while so that Frances and I could spend more time with each other, and from that time we were seldom apart.

Up to the time we became an item it had been my plan to go to California and join my friend John as a saddlemaker, but there's no standing in the way of two young people who are besotted with each other. It wasn't long before we were married.

I soon found out that being mad crazy about each other wasn't enough. I was going to have to do something about making some serious income. I was working in Melbourne at my trade and as well I was doing work for Artransa, a film producing company in NSW, who were making a TV series about stage coaches and Cobb and Co. It was called 'Whiplash' and Peter Graves played the part of Chris Cobb; Peter Armstrong, a rodeo friend, was stuntman and bit player on the show. I had the job of making a bit of gear for them, mainly just strap work, holsters, belts and that type of thing. As well as that, I took on any leatherwork I could find – a bit of saddle work, a handbag for someone in Darwin, some trophy belts for Blackall rodeo.

Stewart the trick rider had visited, we'd talked and designed a few more straps for his saddle. It was only a few weeks later that I got a telegram that read 'Went under the belly today. Stewart'. I don't know what the post-mistress thought, but I knew straight away what it meant. A trick rider performs vaults, drags and stands on a galloping horse. The trick Stewart spoke of in his telegram is when the rider goes down on the near side of the horse, feeds himself headfirst between the galloping legs, reaches through, hauls himself up the off side, and gets back into the saddle again. The 'under the belly' trick was considered the pièce de résistance of trick riding

There was plenty for us to do. We had moved into a new house we'd had built at Bayswater, but it came with no frills. We still had to build paths, a front fence, gardens, a carport and plenty more, but we loved it, it was our home. I had already made the furniture for every room while we were waiting for the builders to finish — a lot of work, but when you're young you can do anything. When we moved in we bought only a fridge, a washing machine and a lounge.

Very soon after moving in, I bought and dismantled for removal a handy sized weatherboard two-stalled stable block. Once I had it reassembled I was able to move my gear from the spare bedroom, and with plenty of room I could do some saddle work.

We'd not been there long when there was talk of a proposed freeway to Healesville. A diagram in the Melbourne paper showed the centreline of this never-to-be-built road going right through our home, from corner to corner. We were tied there; we couldn't sell to anyone except a bloody-minded government department called the Country Roads Board who, after much struggle on our part, offered us a couple of thousand more than we had paid. 'You can take us to court, but we never lose,' was their reply to all our arguments. So we stayed and just went on with our lives, and by 1965 we had three children, Dale, Glenn and Robyn.

I went to a lot of rodeos — not only was I interested in watching, but I had many friends and acquaintances competing. I was still building the trophy saddles for the big annual Mount Isa rodeo.

At the Myrtleford 'Golden Spurs' rodeo I went around behind the chutes to say g'day. After a few familiar hand shakes I saw a young saddle bronc rider I didn't know, he was adjusting his saddle as young bronc riders do. I walked up to him, shook his hand and introduced myself, saying. 'Howdy, I'm Col Hood, the western saddlemaker'. The young guy looked up in total surprise and said. 'Oh! You're Col Hood, I've heard of you for so long I thought you must be an old bloke of seventy five'. That was in 1962, so many years ago. I was certainly well known back then.

Most of the saddles I built then were for calf roping. The Mount Isa trophy saddles were made for roping and were certainly tough – Wally Woods, a top rodeo contestant at the time, told me a story that proved that.

He and a group of rodeo boys were practice roping at Dally Holden's H5U rodeo arena at Townsville when someone said there was a Brahman calf in the chute so fast it was near impossible to rope. Wally, in his Mt Isa saddle and riding a smart bay roping mare named Toots, figured he would prove a point. With his loop built, Wally was ready and waiting; he nodded his head, there was the crash as the chute gates opened, and the calf shot out like a rocket. Toots the mare took off in hot pursuit, but she was due for an abrupt halt. The loop had snagged on a stumpy tree branch next to the chutes, and when the mare ran out of rope she flipped horizontal four feet off the ground. She came back to earth with a deafening thud, but the story ended well. Wally and the horse were OK, that flap-eared calf got away, and the saddle was intact. The only thing broken was the rope.

Graeme Matherick was another rodeo competitor; he was a roper and a part time stunt man and he gave me another example of a good western saddle's strength. As a service to the owner of the cattle used at the rodeo, he was grazing out the beasts on the Cranbourne grass flats, which had been reclaimed from the old Kooweerup and Cranbourne swamplands. Long ago deep ditches had been dug to drain the countryside, and they are retained to keep the land from returning to swampland. The drains are numbered or they have names like 'The Eel Race'.

Graeme was on a Quarter Horse entire called Tonka, and riding in a western roping saddle I had built. He rode the horse down to a big channel to give him a drink, but Tonka tried to walk too far into the water and started to sink in the mud. Being a roper, Matherick carried a calf rope and, thinking quickly, he used the rope to hold the horse's head up and out of the water.

Luckily there was an excavator nearby being used to clean

out the ditches and Matherick signalled the operator to bring his machine over and give him a hand. With a rope fixed to the excavator bucket, Graeme reached down into the water and secured the other end through the handhold on the saddle. This handhold is built into the saddle basically for ease in carrying, but because a good western saddle is built tough, the handhold is equally tough. Before Graeme could ask to have the horse lifted enough to let it scramble its way onto the bank, the operator had hoisted it into the air, swung it around and asked nonchalantly, "Where do you want it?" The operator estimated there was a five thousand pound strain (2270 kg), and those boys know their job.

Since we were so successfully breeding children, I figured it'd be cool to breed a Quarter Horse, and we bought a very nice six-year-old brown mare already in foal. Later that year she dropped a most beautiful filly foal, and I'm sure she was born broken in. We registered and named her Chiquita.

An American, Robert M. Miller, had written a book about 'imprint training', that is handling a newborn foal and imprinting yourself into its mind, and that is exactly what happened with Chiquita. I'm sure she'd read the book. Apart from her mother, I was the first thing she saw. I handled her as soon as she was born and helped her find mum's teat. I'm sure she thought. 'Wow! What a good bloke, he put me onto nice warm milk'. And from that time on, as soon as she spotted me, she'd leave her mum and gallop over for a chat.

For the next couple of years the filly was an endless source of fun for the children and me. As she grew and was weaned she became another household item. I'd look across the paddock and see her lying in the grass with the kids sitting along her back, chattering as kids do.

With Quarter Horses gaining in popularity, a group of us formed our version of a Quarter Horse club and we'd have meetings for the advancement of the newly recognised breed. Since the days of the wild west the Quarter Horse has been bred and developed into a popular, intelligent, extremely agile horse eminently suitable for everything western, as well as for pleasure. The 'quarter' part of the name Quarter Horse came from the original handle, the 'Colonial American Quarter Mile Racehorse'. Two hundred years ago in colonial America, one of the ways the villagers entertained themselves was to run horse races down the main streets, which were usually about a quarter of a mile long, and that accounts for the name. In those times their claim to fame was as sprint racers, and their breeding was held in high esteem.

In 1843 the most celebrated and original Quarter Horse sire was a stallion called Steeldust. His breeding was valued so highly that it was said that if he had even travelled through a district, it was claimed that every foal dropped in the county that year had been sired by Steeldust. In later years the breed took two distinct branches, sprint racing and western riding. It's said the biggest purse for a horse race in the USA is at Ruidoso Downs in New Mexico, and that is a quarter mile sprint race meeting.

Chiquita the filly was the first Quarter Horse I had bred and, as I said, she was born broken in. One day I was walking her through the paddock with my arm over her withers and a halter on her head. She was so quiet and content, I slipped onto her back and she stood quietly; as I urged her forward, she walked on. We enjoyed our very first and most pleasant ride.

A friend had left an open-topped horse trailer at our place so I thought that, while things were going so well, I'd teach her to load. I lowered the tailgate and led her up – and she walked straight in. I looked at her and said, 'How can I teach you to load if you're gonna walk straight in?' So I backed her out and tried again, same result, she walked straight in. Just then Frances called out 'Dinner's ready,' so I put up the tailgate, left her standing there and went in to dinner. When I came back out to check on her, there she was still standing patiently in the trailer, with three or four local kids giggling and sitting along her back. It was a sight to see.

The very next weekend, through our Quarter Horse club, an American friend Charlie Beard was to hold a western horsemanship clinic at Mount Evelyn. I drove Chiquita to the clinic and saddled her for the first time. She accepted it, so I walked beside her for a few yards. She was still looking so at home that I reined her in and quietly stepped aboard. A pat on the side of the neck and I urged her forward; following the other horses, she stepped out into a walk and very soon the activities started. Everybody at the clinic that day found it hard to believe that this was the first time under saddle for the sweet little lady.

It was at Easter in 1968 that I threw in my job at Joe Swift's non-ferrous foundry in Mitcham, Victoria, and started building western saddles full time in my stable block saddle shop at Bayswater.

I was interested in anything western, and had been following reports of Greg Laugher, an American who had decided to bring his horses and settle in Australia. Everything was coming by ship and all the quarantine formalities had been rigorously adhered to, but when the ship docked at Lisbon in Portugal there was a swamp fever scare. The news here was that he had two choices, either throw the horses overboard or spend another six months in quarantine in England. Greg chose the latter option.

He finally settled in Murrurundi, NSW and established a Quarter Horse stud he called Clover Leaf. A guy who was going up there to flog some floats or something asked me if I'd like to go, so I went with him and met Greg and his family. We looked at the horses and he showed me his saddles, which had been made by Earl Naninger in Oakland California. I had taken with me a photo or two of saddles I'd made, and before I left that evening we had arranged a deal where I'd make and supply saddles stamped with a Clover Leaf. That arrangement worked out well; I made a great many saddles with the Clover Leaf mark to order for Greg and his associate over a number of years.

Horses always held a high place in our household. The horses I owned were used either for pleasure or for roping, which was a pleasure. Frances, my other half, chose to follow dressage, a very polished discipline practised widely in Europe. She was dedicated to dressage and was taught by some top instructors. I supported her as we hauled her horses to shows and competitions all around the state.

A few years before I had put a deposit on an eight-acre block that I liked at Yan Yean, and within a week I was offered a couple of thousand more to sell it, but it was such a nice block I wasn't letting it go. With all intentions of relocating, we moved the breeding horses and put them on the good grass on the place. As all horse people do, we cut and baled hay, built a haystack and prepared to build a stable block. At the same time we approached the Country Roads Board for settlement on our home at Bayswater and, as usual, they were downright bloody-minded. With their old taunt of 'take us to court, we never lose,' all we could do was to forfeit the property to them at little more than the original purchase price. With the proceeds we paid the bank out and also the balance on the Yan Yean block. At least that was now ours.

A few years previously I had altered an American saddle belonging to Frank Johnson, a tobacco farmer and owner of Nug Nug ranch, Buffalo River, and had got to knew him fairly well. I was at Myrtleford Rodeo that year, so I drove out along the Buffalo River road to Nug Nug to say hello. I was made welcome and shown the stable block, the Quarter Horses, the stallion and the brood mares with their foals at foot. We talked about saddlemaking and location and I told him of my trouble with the Country Roads mob. That's when he said, 'Come with me,' and we drove up the valley to Lake Buffalo.

'That place is empty,' said Frank, twitching his thumb towards a leased property that fronted the lake. 'You can sell your house and move in here. No rent, just make your saddles and keep an eye on the stock.'

The house at Buffalo River was on the shores of Lake Buffalo. It was big, weatherboard and on two thousand acres of prime grazing land. We had an orchard, a tennis court, hay shed, implement shed, several tobacco kilns and plenty of accommodation. There were two workers' cottages and two single-room bungalows. In front of us the mighty Mount Buffalo was reflected in the placid waters of the lake. Our nearest neighbour was the weir keeper, some two miles away on the other side of the lake and across the dam wall; the next closest was three or four miles further up the valley towards Whitfield.

We pumped drinking water from the crystal clear Croppers Creek into a large tank sitting on top of a nearby hill, that way we had gravity feed. Our electricity was 240 volts from our own Lister diesel generator. When we moved into the house the lighting system was functional and fully automatic – when a light switch was turned on, the generator automatically started, and when the last light was turned off the generator stopped. Cooking was done on a wood-fired range and with bottled gas, we had a gas fridge, and a massive open fireplace to keep us warm in winter.

With all this, and a lot of good friends, the place became a home and we were completely content. We'd found the most perfect place for a young family. There was very poor television reception up the valley where we were, and the big old set we had brought with us didn't work too well. I made enquiries and it turned out that reception in that area was very poor. We discussed all this back home, and when I remarked that we should take the set we had to the rubbish dump and blow it up with a shotgun, the kids, bright-eyed, said, 'Yeah, yeah dad! Let's do it'.

I'm sure it was the best thing we could have done. It gave the kids a whole new direction. There was plenty of things to do and plenty of room to do them in. A lot of reading, and at night we'd sing along or play cards or board games for hours. Nights were dark and very quiet; we all slept well and woke early. Even now I smile to myself to recall putting six-year-old Robyn to bed and a few minutes later have her shuffle in with my guitar. She wanted me to sing her to sleep. Daytimes were always full; we had brought our own horses, our brood mares as well as our saddle horses. I had quickly set up in the garage, which I had converted into a saddle-making workshop. The bigger implement shed at the back is where I set up my bandsaw and vice to make saddletrees.

Very soon after moving in we got to know the weir keeper and his family, a couple of young lads who were completely at home on horseback. When they saw that we were using horses to handle the cattle on the place they offered us the use of a pony so that the kids could learn to ride. The pony, called Cindy, was pretty ordinary looking but it was well behaved. While we had Cindy there, the two youngest kids learned to ride. Glenn was a cowboy and Robyn was becoming a young lady rider. Dale preferred hunting and adventure; he was only mildly interested in horses.

The horse I was riding then was a young Quarter Horse entire I'd bought from a guy I'd made a few saddles for. As soon as I started to ride him I named him Chet after the legendary guitar player Chet Atkins, but he was so good that I gave him the nickname 'Monkey Face'. That was not so much a name as a way of addressing him, like 'C'm on Monkey face, you c'n do it!' I'd use the same handle for anything I liked a lot – a horse, a truck or even, later on, a car.

Chet was great to ride and he loved cattle. I think he considered cattle as lesser beasts and he liked to lord it over them. I'd be moving cattle somewhere with Chet proudly stepping along, and if a beast were to be forward enough to drift the wrong way, Chet would lay back his ears and smartly dive across to head him off at the pass. If the beast took too long, he'd bite it on the bum. None of them ever got past him.

Quarter Horses and western horsemanship were growing all over Australia, and the first Quarter Horse show was held at Moe in Gippsland, Victoria, in 1971, not long after the registry was formed. I was still making saddles for Cloverleaf, and David Briggs, an American, had me make the trophy saddles that were donated to the winners. I took my family along, I think mainly to boost the numbers, but everybody was there; we knew a lot of people and we met even more. We had a good time and I drummed up a heap of saddle work.

I had watched Greg Laugher riding his cutting horse at his Cloverleaf stud, but it was at the Moe Quarter Horse show that I first watched a cutting competition. Feeling how good Chet was under me, I took an interest in the activity and finally Chet and I had instructions in cutting, which was becoming more and more popular.

Chet, AKA Monkey Face, was fun to ride; he'd squeal with excitement and get down nose to nose with the beast. He'd goad it to make a break for it so he could dive across and counter the move. The only thing that might have slowed him down was the rider. I was the one who had to learn; the horse was a natural, he was doing fine. If a rider were to try and tell a cutting horse what to do, it would be too late. He'd have already made his move, and you'd be left sitting in space.

The kids learned to ride on the borrowed pony Cindy, and when the owners took him away we bought another grey pony for them. They called her Misty. We were all so lucky to have so much country to ride; it left us with such wonderful memories. I'd saddle Chet and Misty and we'd ride together through the bushland. Robyn became an accomplished rider; Glenn, who was only mildly interested initially, later developed into a top horseman. As I've said, Dale was more interested in electronics and adventure and just didn't care for horses.

The place was like living in a picture book; it had the bush,

it had the lake and it had Mount Buffalo. Frank Johnson, the friend who had made the place available for us, was so busy as a tobacco farmer, cattle breeder and Quarter Horse stud owner that he never stopped; our place was so restful that he liked to come around just to talk and relax. Sometimes he'd bring his high-profile friends around for a visit, or he'd send them around to see the work I did. They liked to come out into the saddle shop to look at and comment on my work. We'd stand around talking about saddles, horses, the countryside and our lifestyle and very often they'd comment that, in spite of all the trappings of wealth they enjoyed, they really envied our freedom and the way our family lived.

The many freedoms I enjoyed included the times I'd sit and gaze over the lake watching the ducks running frantically over the surface to gain enough momentum for a successful take off. Or I'd wonder as the swans flew in low, letting one wing kiss the water, leaving circles on the mirror-like surface. And as I watched, 'Going Home', the theme from Dvorak's New World symphony, would run through my mind.

CHAPTER 10

Ned Kelly country

One Saturday afternoon a group of us were in the workshop at Mt Buffalo, just standing around talking, when my wife interrupted to tell me the Ambassador to Indonesia was here to see me. As I went out to meet him someone said to Frances, 'Who next? The Queen?'

Waiting to see me were Frank Johnson and Jitno Sukirno, the Ambassador. They wanted to order some leatherwork, waist belts and such. Prior to this visit the President had bought a shipment of Santa Gertrudis cattle from Frank and they were shipped to Bogor in the Java mountains. A short time later Frank gifted the President a Quarter Horse entire named Sundance and, to complete the ensemble, Frank had me make a fully carved western saddle. Shortly after that, Siget, the President's son and his son-in-law, Indra, showed up with their bodyguards and extras. They had come to order fully tooled waist belts, complete with names, but while he was there Siget ordered a western saddle for himself. It was to be fully tooled and he wanted the name of his son Ari carved on the fenders. I did all the work they ordered, sent the belts by mail; and the saddle was picked up by the Ambassador and shipped to Indonesia by diplomatic bag.

Apart from keeping busy making saddles or saddletrees, there was always plenty of maintenance to carry out on a farm like this … pumping water into the tank on the hill, servicing and maintaining the generator, keeping up a stock of firewood. Then there was fishing and hunting to do; shooting rabbits isn't big game hunting, and it's no fun to shoot kangaroos. In the outback it was different, but even out there I'd only shoot by necessity, to feed the dogs or to feed us, never for the fun of it.

This was a cattle property, and soon they wanted us to muster the cattle, to yard them and draft off a mob of good heifers. The safest way to work with Santa Gertrudis is on horseback. Being on foot was bearable, you could get the job done, but the worst thing I encountered was trying to work them with a dog. These cattle are very protective, and at the slightest excuse they'd turn on a dog and send it scurrying off looking for security, maybe behind you. The cow won't mind who she charges … you'll do. And if that looks like happening, it's best to forfeit dignity and head for a fence. But it was good to be back in the saddle doing the same things I'd done back there on the Cooper.

We cut out a mob of fifty odd prime heifers; Frank told me they were for the President of Indonesia and would be flown to Djakarta within ten days. Everything had been arranged, the plane was booked and the flight was scheduled, but there was one big hitch — Frank's son couldn't go, and he was wondering who he could get to take them. I told him not to worry — I had a passport, I knew the cattle, and I'd take them.

We loaded them into a Vickers Viscount propjet that had been specially adapted for carrying livestock – it had been cut in half and twenty feet (7 m) were inserted. The tail section swung to one side to give room to load. We were delayed at Darwin when we stopped to refuel, and by the time we finally left it was one o'clock in the afternoon and the hottest part of the day. The air was very thin, we were fully loaded and going a million miles an hour, the sea was fast approaching and we were still on the ground. I was in the cockpit watching all this and I'm sure I saw the pilot lift the plane bodily by the controls as we finally became airborne and headed for Jakarta.

I was able to stay up front and watch and as I watched, the pilots told me of some of the jobs they had done. Jobs like shipping buffalo from somewhere in Asia to somewhere else in Asia without pens. The landing was so rough that the cockpit ended up full of cattle, and the crew had to exit through the cabin window. They told me another story of when they were transporting elephants in Burma. They had been flying very high and for so long without stopping that when they finally landed there were five tons of frozen elephant urine in the belly of the plane.

It was sundown when we landed, but we couldn't unload until there was a vet check. I was standing in the cabin doorway as they asked me questions from the ground. The temperature in the plane was rising quickly and in reply to the question, 'How many head of cattle are there?' my reply was, 'I've got fifty-one head, but it will be fifty-one dead if we don't get them off soon'. That got things moving; after a cursory vet inspection the tail was opened and the cattle were unloaded and trucked off to their new home at Bogor.

A few days later Siget's driver and bodyguard, Tuan, whom I'd met when they called at our place at Buffalo River, drove me to the farm at Bogor to have another look at the cattle and also to give some hints to the field workers on how to plant tobacco. Along the way he told me that there was a little problem with Sundance, who was getting a bit above himself. When we got to the farm I asked to look at the horse, and when I saw the young boys handling him I said, 'Wow, just ease off a bit with that brush'. Thinking they were helping it, the stable kids were agitating the horse; it had its ears back and was screwing itself away with each stroke they made with the stiff Dandy brush they were using. I showed the workers how to use the softer grooming brushes, and a more relaxing way to use them.

When I said I'd like to give the horse some work, an English saddle and bridle were found in the barn. I saddled him up and went to lead him into the working area – Tuan was right, Sundance was well above himself.

As we approached the gate he tried to charge through in front of me. Quick as a flash I hauled him back and told him in no uncertain terms, 'Stand there and don't move'. I told him to stand still and not to fidget as I walked through the gateway a number of times, then I went back and told him, 'Now walk through beside me with no head shaking and no racing, I want it on a loose lead, you understand?' I was in no hurry, so when I stopped and he walked on, I told him to back up to where he was when I gave the signal. When I had him totally relaxed I decided to mount. I told the horse not to move, and when he moved a foot forward, I pointed and said firmly, 'Put that foot back and don't move it!' It is not what you say that they respond to, it is how you say it, as well as subtle body and hand signals.

I stepped on board and eased him forward. A couple of times around the ménage and we headed out to see the place. After an enjoyable hour or so I headed him back to the stables, where I unsaddled him, washed and dried his back, gave him a feed and brushed him down.

After a few weeks in that busy, crowded land of artists it was time to leave. I'd done all they wanted, Sundance was happy, the cattle had settled in well, so it was off to Bali and then on a Qantas flight to Australia.

It was in 1973 that a phone call brought me the sad news that my friend and mentor, John G. Chirnside, had died of cancer. It grieved me that I had always been so busy working and raising a family that I never got to visit and work with him … let alone play guitar together.

The news set me back a while, but I had to keep working.

He always seemed to be at my elbow just to keep me on the right track, God bless him. There was still plenty to do; Chirnie would be proud.

Myrtleford rodeo is always held on Boxing Day, the day after Christmas, and as usual I took my horse with me – I'd saddle him and ride around to use him as a sort of billboard to let people see what a good western saddle should look like. A good friend, Freddy Hayes was at the rodeo and asked me if I wanted Chet gelded. 'Yes,' I said, 'go ahead. It ain't wise to have an unregistered stallion in a horse breeding area'. Fred, very skilled with horses, was always prepared for any occasion. He gave the horse a twilight shot and very professionally he used the knife while Chet stood there tied to the side of the horse trailer. The horse was standing quietly throughout all this when seven-year-old Robyn walked up. 'What're you doing Mister Hayes?' 'Taking out his tonsils,' replied Fred. 'Gee, they're big tonsils,' said my daughter as she walked off.

When the twilight shot wore off, Fred said to me, 'Just ride him around for a while, he'll be right in a few days'. I took him home, rode him around for an hour every couple of hours, and after a couple of days he was a happy and contented gelding. From then on he was an even more dedicated cutting horse. He only had one handicap … but I was learning all the time.

The new pony was settling in well, and Robyn was encouraged by her mother to prepare for the show ring. She was learning fast, and we were quite proud to see her parading with her ribbons. She looked good amongst the other riders her own age.

We were living well and happily there in the valley, but we were beginning to feel that we should get a place of our own. We figured we'd only buy a property that was just right, so we started scanning the *Weekly Times* for small rural properties, just in case. Then this one came up, a house on almost ten acres, exactly half way between Melbourne and Albury. We drove down and took a look, and we liked what we saw. The auction was to be held on the next weekend at Euroa and we turned up fully intending to buy. The bidding started vigorously, but I stuck at it and was the last man standing. One crack of the gavel and the place was ours.

We now owned a beautiful old brick cottage on the Hume Highway at Balmattum, Victoria. Our house was built from bricks hand fired on the premises; over the past hundred and fifty years more has been added to the original three rooms, making it a perfect home for a family.

The place would have been lived in when Ned Kelly was around; I know he would have ridden past, and most likely called in. One of the banks Ned and his gang robbed was in the nearby town of Euroa. The Faithful family homestead, where the gang divided the booty, was beside Faithful Creek, not half a mile from us. The homestead, that bit of history, was burned to the ground in the huge 1939 bushfires; since then the remaining ruins have been slowly pilfered.

We bought the original settler's homestead of a very large holding. Over the years the original property had been broken up, annexed by family members or sold off to newcomers, which is why we were able to purchase the place. When one local complained about these newcomers moving into the district, my retort was, 'If you don't want us here, don't sell us your bloody land!' But the owners were anxious to sell and we bought the place. No one could have wished for a better location for our interest in horses and my business as a western saddlemaker.

The kids continued their schooling. Our eldest boy, Dale, was an excellent student and followed technical and chemical pursuits; schooling for the younger two was something they did when they weren't with their horses or just mucking around as kids are supposed to do. After erecting a stable block and feed room from an existing hay shed, I helped put up a simple menage for my wife to practise her pursuit of classic dressage.

My riding horse at this time was Chet, the gelding I'd nicknamed Monkeyface.

I would haul him to a friend's place whenever there was cattle work to be done. We'd spend all day mustering or sorting cattle for sale, and at times I'd lend a hand to walk the cattle to the market in Euroa. This type of simple work was good recreational riding, sort of playing at being a cowboy.

Only a few years earlier I had joined in with an arty group in Myrtleford. There I met some wonderful people and I started doing a bit of oil painting as well as sketches in charcoal. I entered a few in competitions, got a few mentions, but never won the big one. That didn't worry me either, I was a saddlemaker not an artist. But now, in our new home in a new location and a new group of friends, I had a whole new lease of life.

To keep my artistic side up I did keep drawing, but mostly I was putting these skills into my saddlemaking. I just wanted to do better and better. The type of leather work I have been doing for over fifty years is called 'leather carving' and most of the artistic work I did was to embelish the magnificent saddles I had made over the years.

Another way of applying this form of art was to make handbags, waist belts, pistol holsters and album covers. I would take on anything that was different, and I was designing and carving superb examples of Indonesian related leatherwork. I had hoped to give a sample of this work to the Indonesian Ambassador I had first met when we were at Buffalo River. Among other things I made a carved collar for Kimba, his little dog, but sadly he was killed in a helicopter crash before he saw the finished work I had done. Once I had started with this very picturesque form of leatherwork, I did some outstanding examples, superb western scene coffee tables as well as accurate carvings in the Egyptian style, carved inwardly and done like the carvings on the pyramids. I was also inspired by scenes of bamboo and water buffalo in Indonesia, as well cameos of Balinese dancers in their beautifully ornate head dresses. Anything I'd draw could be carved into the right type of leather.

I was still doing an amount of leather work for a flamboyant American I had got to know when I was in Buffalo River. He was from from Lubbock, Texas, and his name was Larry Dodson. When I met Larry he was establishing a huge feed lot for beef cattle at Peechelba in north east Victoria. We would visit during the construction, and when the place was full of cattle we'd call in. Larry was quite a dynamo; he'd invite us, we'd stay for dinner and shoot pool.

Larry and I were talking saddles one day when he suggested that I should go over to Texas and work for Windy Ryon in his big saddle store in Fort Worth, Texas. I contacted Windy, the owner, who assured me that as a friend of Larry I was welcome; just come across and I'd be looked after.

Frances was quite content for me to go off and follow my star. I'd talked about it for years and finally my desires, although incomplete, were being fulfilled. The kids were happy for me, and their mother had her horses.

I made the effort and soon I got in contact with Gerard Timberlake, a former customer of John Chirnside. So with Gerard's encouragement and the welcome I'd got from Ryon's, with high hopes I went on my way.

It was 1978, and I spent five months in America on a learning safari combined with a pilgrimage in memory of my old mentor. I spent time at Ryon's, then I travelled the country looking at different saddles, meeting saddlemakers and talking of ways to make my work even better. It is a good thing that I never stopped learning or lost the desire to better myself. I knocked around with cowboys and cowgirls, I did some roping and I rode a top cutting horse.

It saddened me that I was too late to see my old friend John Chirnside. I've never stopped regretting that I didn't make that trip before Chirnie died. While in California I did my best to find Marge, John's widow, but she had moved from their address and I wasn't able to trace her. America, too, is a big counry.

Even in the relatively short time I'd been away the kids seemed to have grown up a lot. Robyn and her mother were doing themselves proud with their beautiful horses, competing in dressage shows around the state. Robyn had trained a very pretty bay galloway she had on loan, with the comment 'Keep her as long as you want her'. Finally she qualified to enter the horse in the equestrian events in the Melbourne Show; they stayed on the grounds to spend as much time as she could preparing for her event. Then the hammer fell. The owner fronted up at the stable block and said, 'I've got some bad news, I've just sold the mare'. That flattened Robyn; she was so proud, and to have that happen was shattering.

Glenn had been working around in different places and he'd had a funny experience when, in an attempt to make some spending money he took on a young horse called Sprocket to break in. He'd saddled the horse, decided to ride him then and there in the back yard, and was all set to mount, when things started to fall apart. The kid missed the mount and the horse threw in a couple of crow-hop bucks, nothing to worry about. Then the resident dog decided to join in the fun and started yapping around Sprocket's feet, which set the horse into some serious bucking. Soon he'd bucked under the clothes hoist, got the rotary bit caught in the saddle horn and, still bucking, lifted the hoist and the week's washing right off the pole. Urged on by the frantic barking of the dog, and still wearing the clothes hoist, Sprocket bucked across the yard to make a break for freedom down the driveway. The trouble was that the driveway was blocked by a car parked half way along, but that didn't daunt Sprocket. He bucked relentlessly on, got himself and the clothes line

 three quarters of the way through the gap between the car and the house and then got stuck, draped in a floral bed sheet and looking foolish. He was extricated without too much drama. Glenn went on to become a very proficient horseman and cutting horse trainer.

Our eldest son, Dale, was travelling the country working and looking for adventure. He had learned a trade as a welder and could earn a living anywhere, but he was living at home for a while until his Yamaha motorcycle was repaired. He worked night shifts in Benalla and rode Robyn's boy friend's motorbike to work.

It was in October 1983 that the world as our family had always known it came crashing down. You're sure you are made of good, resilient well-seasoned timber, but you never forget the shock when the police knock on the door and say, 'We've bad news for you, there's been an accident, it's your son Dale'. They seemed to let it out slowly.

'Is he badly hurt?'

'We're sorry to report, he's dead.'

Glenn was a rock at that time. He made all the funeral

arrangements, contacted all Dale's friends and did everything that needed to be done.

It's a big chunk out of your life when you lose a child. Throughout your life, your inner being sort of resigns itself to the fact that after your parents go, you're the one who's supposed to go next. If it's your kid, you can't swap places, even though you'd like to. It's a thing you just have to accept. I left the porch light burning as a beacon, and it stayed on until the bulb finally burned out.

In some strange way we had to go on. I sold my saddle horse Alphabet and that provided some working capital. To keep my mind as straight as I could, I bought another horse, a Quarter Horse gelding named Doc's Legend. He was a well built palomino, complete with wavy flowing mane and a tail that reached the ground. Having a friend like Doc close at hand helped me immensely; he was something warm and friendly. With the help of some good guitar-playing friends and the warmth of a pal like Doc I finally begun to get myself together. I had a bit of work and I always tried to meet my promised dates for delivery. I still had a living to earn and commitments to meet.

Talking about promised delivery dates, at the time of Dale's death I had a saddle started and had promised delivery the next week. I have no interest in remembering who those people were, but when I phoned to tell them what had happened and that it would take another couple of weeks to get the saddle finished, their response was a vehement 'No! You promised it in a week's time, and we want it then'. I have no idea how the saddle looked when it was finished; it's hard to do beautiful work when your eyes keep welling. But I got the job done in a week, and when they picked the saddle up I told them, 'Just don't ever come to me wanting another saddle'.

Life had a hollow ring. My wife Frances was spending a lot of time with her horses and other friends, Glenn was now

living in Lilydale with his girl friend Vikki, and Robyn was
living the other side of Euroa and preparing to get married.
For the first time in my life I didn't have much bloody work
on hand, and I seemed to be rattling around in that big old
house.

It was then that number two son said he had found a shop
in Lilydale and that I should move there to live and work. It
seemed a good idea at the time so I did just that, I rented the
shop. Work was low, so I advertised a couple of saddles I had,
and they went quickly. With other enquirers I just told them
that those two saddles were sold but I could make for them
just what they wanted. That way I was back on my feet again.
I did some beautiful work there, all made to order.

On the weekends I'd drive to Euroa to do maintenance
and to be at home with what was left of my family. Then my
daughter Robyn and her guy, Milton, wished to get married.
As I was living in Lilydale, I asked them to make all the
arrangements and I'd be proud to pick up the tab and give
my daughter away.

The wedding went well. It was in the park, and the whole
town turned out to watch as the wedding party arrived in a
pair of buggies drawn by beautifully presented horses. I hired
a set of tails, but when it came to shoes Robyn was insistant.
'You'd better buy a new pair of cowboy boots,' she said, 'I've
never seen you in shoes'. I bought black, Cuban heeled Tony
Lama, which set off the grey dinner suit and tails well.

It was not long after that I learned my marriage was, like
the wreck of the Hesperus, on the rocks, wrecked, kaput.

I know that going through a trauma like Dale's death put
an incredible strain on the relationship, and I'm sure that,
although I was behaving in a manner that I thought was
right, I was probably being a total jerk. I guess I must have
screwed up, too, by living away for a spell and not being with
the family. I was to find out that in that short time, somebody
else had provided solace. Although our marriage was not one

of those made in heaven, it was a shock to be told that it was over.

I had no need for a store front, so the next day I gave up the lease and spent a couple of weeks making saddles in the stable of a friend in Coldstream. That was OK for a while, until I found my feet again.

That's when, with the help of a dear friend in Wandin, Victoria, I started working in a big packing shed on the place. I was never alone there; ain't that strange? There were so many women around – some seemed crazy and others *were* crazy, but I had what I needed, and that was company. I was working hard, not eating well, and within a week of starting work in the barn a girl came into my life. I rented a house and we moved in; I figured that way I would at lest eat well. She seldom showed up, and It took a little while for it to sink in that she was one of the crazy ones. We didn't last long as an item, and I told her I was giving up the house. I cleaned out the loft above my saddle work area and moved in there. It was the second artist's garret I had lived in.

The loft was unlined, drafty, cold and it swayed in the strong southerly winds that blew relentlessly. I just kept working automatically, I had no interest in eating, but I didn't let the booze get to me. Every now and then a few horse friends would bring a couple of six-packs and we'd drink beer, talk horses and discuss all the usual crap. I went out a lot, dated a few women, but there was a big hole in my life. I decided that what I needed was an overseas change. That's what I'd do, I'd head for Canada and a new way of life.

I had been laid very low in Australia, the land I love, and I needed that move to help me rebuild my life. People would ask 'Why Canada?' My stock reply was, 'Because you can't go any further without being on your way back again!'

I would be away for four years.

CHAPTER 11

Born lucky

I guess I'd been away long enough. My daughter said she missed me, and that made me think of Australia. She told me that she had called into a saddle shop in Melbourne and asked if they had any Col Hood saddles. They told her, 'No, they're very rare, he's dead you know'. Robyn was set aback, and replied, 'I didn't know that, and I don't think he even knows it himself'. She went on, 'I'll tell dad next time I phone him'. It was time I went back and proved these untimely rumours wrong.

I didn't realise that I had lost my Australian accent until I arrived at Sydney airport. The accent of the airport staff sounded so broad to me that I was astounded, but then I had never been away for so long and spent so long without hearing another Australian. At Tullamarine I was greeted by Robyn, and as we walked to the car I was struck by the familiar smell of gum trees

Now that I was back, what the hell was I gonna do? I stayed with Robyn for a few weeks and borrowed her car to become re-acquainted with a few old friends. I wasn't mad keen to get back to saddlemaking; that was something I could always fall back on. I had some US currency left so I bought a car, an HQ Holden station wagon I called the love machine, and drove around Victoria just for a nostalgic look. At Balmattum I stopped and found the house was empty; divorced and now remarried, Frances was living in another town. The old pioneer cottage was still in my name, so I chose to live in it. The house was 150 years old, it felt sad and lonely, so I opened it up and let the air in. Then I decided to do as much of a full make-over as I could.

I have a knack of falling on my feet. Way back I had a wonderful lady friend who would say, 'Better to be born lucky than rich,' so I've always chosen to consider myself 'born lucky'. I cashed in a policy that afforded me the money to do a bit on the house, and I was wondering what to do to earn a dollar when the phone rang. It was the artist Hugh Sawrey, 'Good day Colin, this is Huey, can you make me a saddle?' I thought, 'Well here's someone who doesn't think I'm dead'. 'G'day Huey,' I answered, 'yes sure, what sort?' 'A cutting saddle,' he replied, 'I'm gonna take up cutting'. I built his saddle, and that started the whole thing over again. I got some saddle repair work as well, and that kept me going.

It was then that I started to settle in as an Australian. The years in North America had worked wonders for me. I was so long in there that sometimes I'd forget that I was Australian until someone would say 'I love your accent, I wish I had an accent'. I'd say to them, 'You do! You have a strong accent'. 'Yes, but not like yours!' they'd say, and so it would go on.

Americans like Australians, and my Australian accent had helped me make a lot of friends, although it was not only through my accent that I got talking to people. One evening in the bar I spoke to a young fellow sitting alone at a table and he indicated to me that he was deaf. I went behind the bar, grabbed a pad and pen and I asked him his name. He wrote down 'Delbert'. I bought a couple of beers and we had a long conversation using the pad and pen. He was interested in the fact that I was saddlemaking in town and he asked if there was any way he could help me in the saddle shop. I said that he could call in and I was sure there was plenty he could do. I knew that I had some repair work; he could pull those saddles to pieces and we could take it from there. Well, he showed up and I wrote down what I wanted him to do, but I soon found that written conversations were laboriously slow and frustrating. So in the next note I wrote, 'This is too bloody slow, teach me to sign and we'll get on a lot better'.

The first signs I learned were the alphabet, Delbert's name sign and the signs for horse, a saddle and the sign for work. Delbert started coming in quite often.

I was learning sign language well and very soon I got to know a married couple, Ted and Joanne Beery, who were both deaf. They started showing me more signs, until quite soon I could carry on a conversation. Most of the talk is in signs, very little is spelled out letter by letter.

In America I never heard one bad word about Australia or Australians. Older guys who had fought with our troops in World War II couldn't speak highly enough of them. Younger kids from the cattle ranches wanted to experience the outback. My biker friends were taken with the television persona Harry Butler reaching under a rock and holding out his hallmark handful of scorpions. Most of the people I met had dreams of visiting the 'land down under'.

There were times when I wished we could be more polite to visitors, especially from America. In 1990 I had not long been back and was driving around the state when I called in to visit Sovereign Hill in Ballarat. The last time I had been there was when the kids were young. Dressed in casual western clothes, I walked around looking at the features and got interested in a huge beam pump; I think it was a working exhibit. Seeking a bit more information, I tried to get into conversation with a young attendant but she was quite off handed and couldn't be bothered to speak. Set back at her attitude, I said to her, 'I've got gold in me blood, I was born not far from here in Daylesford; my dad was a gold miner'. She looked at me and said, 'You're Australian are you?' I replied 'Yes, I'm Australian and proud of it.' 'Oh! then I'll speak to you,' she said.

After the way I was accepted in America, I was ashamed of the attitude of that girl, whose job it was to talk to tourists and make them feel welcome. But I didn't let that get to me;

even with a residual Nebraska accent, I found most people polite and willing to talk.

I did miss having a horse under me, and here my luck worked again. The phone rang and it was Vikki, my son Glenn's old girlfriend. 'Do you want Doc back?' she asked. 'Doc's Legend' was the superb palomino Quarter Horse gelding I had bought from a Swan Hill stud in the early eighties, and had left in the hands of Glenn and his girlfriend when I went overseas. Somehow he ended up belonging to Vikki.

Vikki went on to tell me that Doc was crippled and couldn't be ridden, but he could make a good house pet. I figured I'd go down to Lilydale and pick him up; at least I would give him a good home. When I got there to collect him he was in superb condition, he looked a million dollars. Vikki told me that he was crippled and two vets had told her he could never be ridden again. She told me they thought it might help if they removed his patellas (knee caps).

As I was loading him to take him home I thought, 'What a lot of crap, I'll take him round to Ellis Thompson and see what he thinks'. I drove the few miles around to Wandin, where my old horse chiropractor friend lived, and as I was backing the horse out of the float Ellis said, 'Well, there's nothing wrong with the rear end. Now we'll look at the front end'. He found that a main tendon had slipped from behind the elbow and was running down the outside of the shoulder. That must have been from the time the silly goat got hung up trying to jump out of a set of yards when I first brought him down from Euroa in 1985. Ellis showed me what he was doing, and with a 'twang' he popped the tendon back in place.

Things were really looking up. Now I had a home, a car and, thanks to Ellis, I had my saddle horse back again. Doc was as sound as a bell. My life was starting to reform, and in the house I even found the guitar I had bought when I was in the barn. Months earlier I had made a western saddle and sent it from USA to Australia. It hadn't arrived and I thought it was lost, but it finally turned up at the local depot. So now I had one of my own saddles, branded 'Made in America'.

At this time I was able to buy a current model Mazda ute, and my son Glenn and I built a two-horse 'fifth wheel' gooseneck trailer to fit. Now I had a home base, a guitar, a new saddle and a superb riding horse as well as a ute and trailer. I was totally free to go wherever I wanted. Born lucky! I could do just what I pleased.

I'd haul Doc around the state in my gooseneck and set up camp. Then I'd saddle up and ride for the sheer pleasure of being alone in the Australian bush with a good reliable friend like Doc. I had learned from experience that you always look after your horse first, then you think of yourself. In the outback all those years ago I learned that if you wanted to stay alive, you made sure you kept the horses alive. All those miles I had covered as a young restless kid, and all the experiences, had made all that automatic.

Nothing was any trouble, everything worked. I was quite content in my gooseneck. I got an easy pleasure camping alone in the bush, with Doc tethered nearby on good grass. I even got to enjoy the inevitable chomp, chomp, chomp.

For twenty years one of my absolute pleasures was to haul a horse off to NSW and spend a few days helping a drover friend shepherd out and walk a mob of cattle to graze on the roadside. Although the councils in Victoria had outlawed the practice of moving cattle by foot, it was still done over the border. It was a good way to give experience to the new young Quarter Horse mare I'd just bought. She was Peppy Snake bred and called Miss Cutter Could (Missy). She was as attractive as Doc, another palomino with the same rich golden coat and the same full snow-white wavy mane and tail. They made a beautiful matching pair.

There is nothing like the pleasure of spending day after day on a good reliable horse as you either move a huge mob of cattle to a holding paddock or just sit and watch them graze. But that's not all that can happen. All those years ago we had talked about it, but I never experienced a 'stampede' or a 'rush' in the outback… it was in NSW on one of those relaxing weekends that I finally saw it happen.

We'd camped the cattle, a mixed mob of a full thousand head, in a seemingly secure spot on the roadside five miles from a small southern NSW country town. The mob was enclosed against a sound eight-strand barbed wire fence on one side, with a single electric 'hot wire' to hold them and the horses in place. It was about two in the morning when we heard a loud all-encompassing 'whoosh'… in an instant the entire mob was at full rush. A good half went galloping blindly towards Walbundrie, a town up the road a few miles, while the other half went through the barbed wire fence into an unoccupied paddock of about 500 acres (200 hectares).

We were on our feet in an instant. Steve the drover, who knew the area, leapt into his ute and was off to stop them before they reached the town. The other guy and I leapt into the Mazda and, with the gooseneck, we drove to where Steve had stopped the cattle. While Steve went to find the horses, we guarded the road to warn any motorists who might come along, and I made some coffee and a feed while we waited for daylight. Then we'd be able to see what the hell we were doing and could pick up the pieces. When Steve came back with the horses, we saddled up and mounted, ready to put the mob back together again.

That event showed me what could have happened in the outback, in that untamed land way beyond the fences. With some of those wild free-running station cattle and equally ill-mannered horses, we could have taken a week to get the mob back on the trail again. I was pleased that my only experience with a stampede ended so easily.

It looked to us like a mob of kangaroos had spooked the cattle, and in their rush they'd taken the horses with them. We gathered the cattle on the road and walked them back to the campsite; Steve grazed these out while the other bloke and I collected the cattle that had crashed into the paddock, and we walked these down to re-form the mob. After all that, there was not a beast injured in any way and, as a bonus, two cows had calved in the middle of all that ruckus.

We held the mob in the same place the next night and they camped quietly. There were travelling stock reserves in the area, but in its dubious wisdom the council had leased them out to the football club to graze sheep. When I asked Steve, 'Whose cattle are these?' his cynical reply was, 'You know that councillor who wanted roadside droving outlawed?' I said 'Yeah!' and he replied. 'Well these are his bloody cattle, he has no pasture. Ain't it ironical?' Just goes to show you, we've all got our place.

You have to make money, even if it is just enough to get by. Hugh Sawrey, good friend and bushman, once said to me, 'Always carry a few paintbrushes with you, that way you can make a living doing a bit of signwriting.' That advice came in handy in America, where they hold anyone with talent in good stead. I'd paint for them and they'd pay. Not a lot...but I didn't ask a lot.

It was while I was doing one of these signwriting jobs that Ranny Florae showed up. He was a Louisiana Cajun leatherworker I'd met back in 1978. We became good friends, we'd make music together, and he'd show me runs on the guitar. In the past he'd played with country entertainer Faron Young, but since then he'd fallen on hard times. If ever he was a bit short of money I'd buy him a drink and something to eat. The guitar he owned was a beautiful hollow box Gibson; I offered to buy it but he wouldn't sell. He held that with it he could always earn a feed…or at least he could get a drink.

It was for a bottle of rye whiskey that some low-life suckered out of Ranny a letter from Buffalo Bill Cody. A short time later Lowlife sold the letter at auction for five thousand dollars, and didn't give the old boy a cent. I didn't want Ranny's guitar to sell, just to play. But I didn't depend on my guitar for a feed, and drinking never interested me that much.

I tried a little street busking, it was a bit of fun, I made a few dollars but that wasn't going anywhere. I wasn't real good at busking, but I was with my saddle work. I called myself the 'Saddle Tramp', just another campfire singer. I liked to play and sing a bit of western to entertain myself and a few friends. It was my leatherwork that earned me a living.

I lived alone for a while at Balmattum, and when I wanted to get out for a break I'd load Doc into my gooseneck and head off for a few days. My fifth wheel was not only a horse float, it was a self-contained camper trailer complete with sleeping area over the sticking out bit in the front. I also carried horse feed, a stove, cooking gear, dishes, a table and chairs, everything I needed. I would drive to a place that I knew was good horse-riding country, find a nice secluded area of bushland that was near water, and make camp. Maybe I'd go to Daylesford, where I'd take the waters, or maybe Bright or the Buckland Valley. Although I carried horse feed, I liked to be on a bit of picking for the horse, so that he could be left and wouldn't be bored. I'd saddle up and go riding just for the pleasure, or I'd leave the horse on the tether, unhook the trailer and drive into town and call on one of the real estate agents. I'd say I was thinking of selling up and buying a place in the area, and if he was keen to make a sale he'd show me around to look at properties. That way I'd see the countryside, and when I'd seen enough I'd go back to Doc and my trailer and return home. No way did I want to leave the prettiest little place in the state.

In those first couple of years back in Australia I made some nice cutting saddles. Cutting is that horse sport where the rider walks the horse into a herd of cattle in an arena and quietly guides the horse to pick out one beast and walk it away from the rest of the cattle. This is where the action starts. The beast will instinctively try to get back with the rest of the cattle, and the horse will keep it out. In a cutting competition, you are not allowed to guide the horse in any way, and it is an amazing fact that if you do anything to try and help the horse, you are in the way. You are half a second too late and you're putting the horse off. At times I found I was tending to use the reins and the horse was unsure of what I wanted, so I just took off the bridle.

With good cutting breeding, Quarter Horses have the same instinct as a good sheep dog, it comes naturally. When cutting a beast from a mob you can urge the horse on with your body movement, and you can easily guide it without reins by the way you use your legs; point your right foot and it will go right, etc. Once you have let the horse know which calf you want, just sit tight … you're on a tornado. When you want it to stop, lightly pinch its mane and he'll quit and walk away. I left the bridle off all day.

There is nothing like the buzz of sitting on half a ton of animated dynamite, being nose to nose with a beast on a horse that is quicker and more agile than a cat playing with a mouse. I got a lot of pleasure out of the sport of cutting, as well as getting a lot of saddle work. The thing that put me off was the cost of training, as well as the 'cattle hire' and the entry money. The training and travelling sort of cut into my time. I had other things to do.

In fact the time had come for me to do some serious forward planning. Having fun with the horses was all right for a while, but I was still behaving a bit like an overgrown kid. It was time I settled down.

Then my lucky streak cut in again. One day in 1993 Mary knocked on my door. with a broken halter to be repaired. She'd not long moved from Shepparton, Victoria and was here, not far from me, to help out her sister on her agistment farm. With a smile she handed me the halter, and as I replaced the straps and sat there hand sewing them we talked and joked together. We hit it off well and, without my knowing it, Mary had fallen for me. A few days later, and quite by happy accident, we met again. Pleased to see each other, we talked and I asked her out to dinner. Not being from the district she said, 'Where do you go around here?' My reply was, 'I dunno, but come to my place and I'll cook a beautiful meal for two'.

From that time on we started spending time together, enjoying each other's company. We became a couple. We'd sing together, we'd laugh a lot. We were soul mates, two people made for each other, and we lived in perfect harmony.

Over the years I'd made a lot of saddles for working cattle stations, and now I'd been invited to spend time on Carbeen station, one of those big cattle exporters out of Katherine in the top end.

'Go,' said Mary, 'go and have fun. These chances don't come up every day'.

So, with Mary's blessing, I went.

Darwin Airport was vastly different from the last time I was there in 1973 with the plane-load of cattle for Indonesia.. Since then Cyclone Tracy had blown the town and the airport clean away. The station owner, John Quintana, was waiting at

the posh new terminal, and that same afternoon he flew us
to the home station in a light plane. Looking down on that
vast country again did my heart good. So did the hospitality
at the homestead.

The cattle they run up there now are 'Bos indicus'.
Originating in the Indian subcontinent, these super tough
grey-coated, flap-eared Brahman types were bred to handle
severe sunlight and extreme tropical heat, vastly superior
to the Hereford-shorthorn cross types we worked back in
the fifties. The Quarter Horses used on the place were bred
and broken in on the station, and they preferred to use the
American roping saddle. That suited me fine; I'd been making
them for the past fifty years.

No mucking about there, we were up next morning at the
crack of dawn and ready to start work. I was was given a
horse with the seemingly peculiar name of Big Enough, after
the story 'Big Enough', by old time American cowboy artist
and author Will James. A lot of my love of the American
west came from a Will James book given to me by John
Chirnside back in 1958. The wonderful drawings and the
stories, combined with my own inborn love of the outback,
gave me something that has always stayed with me. As for
Will James, it's said that although his mistress was whisky,
his true love was the west.

Sitting there on Big Enough, doing the same job I'd done
way back in time, my mind drifted back to what I'd learned
over the years. Read the mob, look to each side as well as
watching the ones straight ahead and, just like I learned back
then, keep the mob together looking neat and tidy.

A big shipment of export beef cattle was to be loaded the
next day, and we had a big area to muster. I was to ride in the
helicopter; my job was mainly as gate opener and closer. I'd
reckon that, as a guest, I was given that task just for the thrill
of it.

As we worked, the pilot would drop down and land,

I'd jump out and open the gate, climb back in and we'd go back up. There were no doors, so I'd try to grab a handful of leaves as we skimmed the tree-tops. After we'd located and gathered in a bunch of cattle, the pilot would fly the chopper on its edge and use the dust from the downdraft to keep them moving. With good keen eyesight, one of us would see a rogue steer skulking in the brush, acting the same as the rogue beasts I'd encountered fifty years ago. They'd skulk down and hide, you'd ride in close to move them, and that's when they'd come up under your horse snorting, and lift him off the ground. A lot better in a helicopter – the pilot would dart back, get above the beast and drive him back into the mob, and run them all through the gate. He'd drop down, I'd jump out, shut the gate, and we'd be off again.

Stockmen on horseback were doing the ground work; we'd keep in touch with them using phones linked by satellite. Now and then we'd drop down to parlay and coordinate plans. These places are huge, but they still have paddocks and boundary fences. Over the boundary is another equally vast cattle empire with the same wiry, tough stockmen. Mostly they'd be on horseback, sometimes on motorcycles, and of course when the water buffalo run free, there were the 'bull catchers' in their tough, battered Toyotas.

But none of that on Carbeen. There wasn't a motor bike on the place – you rode horses. This was John Quintana's way. There was outrage when he advertised for stockmen, stipulating that western saddles would be used and rolled up shirt sleeves would be not be tolerated. It seems there were people who claimed it was 'un-Australian'. I dunno what that means; the horses were well mannered, well fed and well turned out, the western saddles used were well suited for the task. I guess it took a little time to get used to working with their shirt sleeves rolled down, but the stockmen did look tidy.

At times the work was full on; one morning we were up, fed and mounted by five in the morning. We had twelve hundred head of beef cattle to muster, draft, weigh and load into road trains. That's a lot of cattle, and everything we did was on horseback. We'd move them from the bigger holding paddocks to smaller yards, where the export beasts were finally drafted. These cattle were then weighed and moved forward towards the loading chutes, where workers on foot would urge them up into the double-decked multi-trailer trucks

We worked from first light until all the trucks were loaded and on their way to Darwin. At about two in the afternoon we knocked off, had a meal and rested for a couple of hours, but we were mounted, ready and waiting to load the rest when the first of the trucks returned. I felt good as I worked on horseback, pushing up, drafting and gathering more cattle until the last truck was loaded and on the track. This is fast, hard work; there is no room for fools or drongos. You need to do the work willingly, and if you do screw up, listen, learn and do it right next time.

It was well after sundown when we walked the horses to the yards, unsaddled them, wiped down their backs, watered and fed them ... as always, look after your horses first and then think of yourself. After the saddles were put away, the tack room swept and the chores were done, we sat in the yard with a few Melbourne Bitters while the boss cooked up barbecued beef. We sat around then and talked cattle, horses, saddles and the kick of helicopter mustering until we finally drifted off to our bunks.

Next morning we flew to another of the stations for a look around, and a look around we certainly had. A photographer was travelling with us and he wanted to get some publicity

shots of the station from the air. It was quite a flight – just stand the plane on its edge so we can look straight down, and listen to the machine gun staccato clicks of the camera shutters. After a quick meal we drove out to visit the crew at their cattle camp, right in the middle of nowhere.

It could have been a scene straight out of 'The Overlanders' or 'Lonesome Dove' ... the saddles resting on rails, the horses grazing close at hand, the men sitting around checking gear and talking. At the same time the sweaty cook in his shirt sleeves and apron was fussing about the stove making a pot of stew. Those outback cooks haven't changed much, it's only the cooking gear that's been upgraded. Just as it was fifty years ago, camp cooks themselves still can be either cooks, cuckoos, grub spoilers or just crazy. This one looked as though he might even be a cook.

Looking down on Australia's ancient landscape on the flight back to Melbourne, I thought back to the time when it was all new to Spinifex Mick and me as we travelled north with our wagon and our horses. This is where our dreams were headed, although the big 1956 floods put an end to that. But I knew that I still loved this vast timeless land with the same intensity I had when I was young and wide-eyed.

It belongs to us all, and it should remain what it is, the plains of God.

Epilogue

For me there's nothing like the comforting touch of a horse's muzzle to calm the soul, and there have been times when I've desperately needed it. For someone born lucky, I have had the emotional crap knocked out of me a few times. On the other hand, there are rich memories and new pursuits …

Mary and I reckoned we had it made; we were totally devoted to each other. She not only loved me, but she truly loved my horses. Doc was the world's most gentle horse and he'd be quite the gentleman with Mary on his back. Arthritis finally made it too painful and she had to stop riding, but it still gave her lasting pleasure to be with the horses. We had a million friends; everybody loved her. She'd tell them all that she was my biggest fan, and that her life started when she met me. I'll be ever grateful for those wonderful years we spent together.

Mary had it tough in the last few years. Worsening arthritis gave her constant pain, and in the latter months of 2008 it caused an ulcer to form under the ball of her foot. I bathed and dressed it constantly but it got no better – it was infected with golden staph. She had contracted that bloody foul contagion after a serious back operation two years earlier, and now it had re-emerged.

On Australia Day of 2009 Mary was admitted to hospital. With all the hope in the world I'd visit, we'd talk and make plans, but she was always tired. A week later I sat by her bedside, held her hand and watched her die. With misty eyes I said *Vaya con dios, Mary mi amore*. Go with God, Mary my love.

Losing Mary, I lost half of my life … the good half. Losing

my son, Dale, broke my heart. The unstoppable Spinifex Mick was laid low by lung cancer – Mary was taken aback by the number of friends we met at the service. Big ten-foot-high Mack, the mighty blacksmith, died of hard work and old age.

There is a poem by the great cowboy singer and raconteur, Don Edwards (Thirty Years a Buckaroo) about putting off visiting an old friend until it is too late. You get word that the friend has died and, like the song says, you are left thinking, 'I really should have gone …' That sums up Chirney and the guitar. I've never forgotten a thing I learned from him, nor a word he said. I am happy to pass on anything he taught me to anyone who, like me all those years ago, will look, listen and learn.

Maturity has helped me slow down my carefree and adventurous ways. No more grabbing bulls by the tail like we did in the days of the intrepid Spinifex Mick – capers like that are for the young and crazy like Mick and I were. But how lucky am I to have a whole hatful of those good times to look back on and relish!

Some years back I lost my trusty friend Doc, and I sold my cutting mare, Missy, with foal at foot. But should I choose to 'go bush' on horseback for a few hours, there are lots of friends who will stick a good horse under me. There is an old saying 'a cowboy never sells his saddle', but the saddle a saddlemaker is riding in is always for sale. It happens I'm an old cowboy, too, so I kept one saddle.

Here in the peace and tranquillity of 'Sweet Home Balmattum' I get a lot of pleasure from drawing and writing stories and illustrating for horse magazines, but I haven't totally left the world of western saddles – now I'm writing about them. My first book on the subject, *The Western Saddle Handbook* was very successful; now I'm writing another, to be called *Making a Western Riding Saddle*.

My tack room, where I've always kept my horse gear for security and safety, has now become a storehouse of great memories. On the floor, my shoeing gear sits patiently waiting to be used again, but my original 'hatful of nails' got itself rained on, the nails rusted, and the hat was chucked out. A well travelled cowboy hat rests comfortably on the horn of my good western saddle.

Everything's OK.

Time to call it a day. Thanks for your company, I hope you enjoyed the ride. Maybe we'll saddle up again some time. There's still a lot of country to cover.

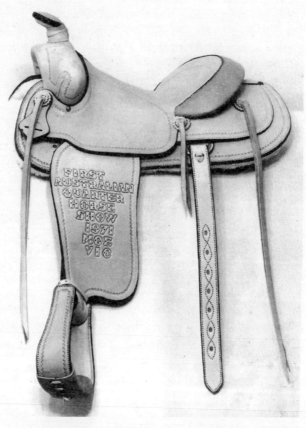

The tack room is the repository of my memories..

Index